The Stony Ground
The Remembered Life of
Convict James Ruse

Christine & Rick,
June 2018.

Michael Crowley

≋ WATERSIDE PRESS

The Stony Ground: The Remembered Life of Convict James Ruse
Michael Crowley

ISBN 978-1-909976-57-3 (Paperback)
ISBN 978-1-910979-57-0 (Epub E-book)
ISBN 978-1-910979-58-7 (Adobe E-book)

Cover design © 2018 Waterside Press by www.gibgob.com. Sketch and description of the Settlement at Sydney Cove, Port Jackson in the County of Cumberland taken by a transported convict on the 16th of April, 1788, which was not quite three months after Commodore Phillip landed there, courtesy of the National Library of Australia.

Printed by Lightning Source.

Main UK distributor Gardners Books, 1 Whittle Drive, Eastbourne, East Sussex, BN23 6QH. Tel: +44 (0)1323 521777; sales@gardners.com; www.gardners.com

North American distribution Ingram Book Company, One Ingram Blvd, La Vergne, TN 37086, USA. Tel: (+1) 615 793 5000; inquiry@ingramcontent.com

Australian distribution Waterside Press can arrange local delivery in Australia for any customers unable to source books direct from Ingrams there.

Cataloguing-In-Publication Data A catalogue record can be had from the British Library.

e-book *The Stony Ground: The Remembered Life of Convict James Ruse* is available as an ebook and also to subscribers of Ebrary, Ebsco, Myilibrary and Dawsonera.

Published 2018 by
Waterside Press Ltd
Sherfield Gables
Sherfield on Loddon, Hook
Hampshire RG27 0JG.

Telephone +44(0)1256 882250
Online catalogue WatersidePress.co.uk
Email enquiries@watersidepress.co.uk

Table of Contents

Acknowledgements

The Stony Ground received time to write support from Arts Council England, and I would particularly like to thank my mentor, Andy Croft. His guidance, editorial support and encouragement helped the development and completion of this book. There are too many invaluable sources of research to mention in full, but I must express my thanks to Janice Ruse Huntington for her short book *My Mother Reread Me Tenderly: The Life of James Ruse* (Possum, 1988), in which she gathered and presented all official records pertaining to her ancestor. I would also like to thank the staff at the Mitchell Library, Sydney, who were so helpful during my research.

Michael Crowley
West Yorkshire, June 2018

Preface

James Ruse, born 1759, was a Cornish farm labourer who at the age of twenty-three was sentenced to seven years' transportation to New South Wales for stealing two silver watches. He was one among the eight hundred or so convicts shipped by the First Fleet to Botany Bay in May 1787. He became, arguably, the most important convict of that fleet or any other.

He was the first European ashore in January 1788, carrying the officers onto the beach, among the first convicts emancipated, and the first individual to be given a land grant on the continent. He was Australia's first self-sufficient farmer, his land ownership placing him at the apex of a conflict with indigenous peoples which on the Hawkesbury River escalated to a war.

Whether it was fortune or design that put James Ruse at so many significant moments of the infant colony, he was also cursed by man and nature. He was reduced, as he would have seen it, to years of perilous seal-hunting along the coasts of New South Wales and New Zealand, including a mysteriously ill-fated expedition aboard the *Speedwell* in 1805. While there are many remarkable convict stories from the First Fleet his life more than most was lived at the frontier of history, his own survival bound-up with the fate of the colony itself.

Today in Parramatta, New South Wales, there is a seven kilometre long highway and a high school named after James Ruse. There is not much in the way of biography to be found though, for the world of a convict settler was not a recorded one. What follows is a fictionalised account constructed around the historical records; it is James' story to himself, in his own words: the voice of one of England's rural poor, common land enclosed, sent across the world to enclose the land of others. It is one of many lost voices and it calls-out to be re-imagined.

About the author

Michael Crowley is a writer and dramatist who has worked in theatre, youth theatre, prisons and, most recently, with the British Army. He lives in West Yorkshire.

Also by Michael Crowley:

Drama *The Man They Couldn't Hang* (Waterside Press)

Poetry *Close to Home; First Fleet*

Non Fiction *Behind the Lines: Creative Writing with Offenders and People at Risk* (Waterside Press)

Fiction *Nowhere to Run*

You can find out more about his work at www.michaelcrowley.co.uk

'Another colonial sealing vessel, the *Speedwell* of eighteen tons owned by John Grono, a name afterwards to be famous in New Zealand sealing, had been stranded in October 1804. She was got off by Andrew Thompson the ship owner, and in the second week of August, 1805, he sent her on a sealing expedition to the coast of New Zealand. From this voyage, she returned in September 1806, fairly successful in procuring seals, but unfortunate in losing three men. The scene of the catastrophe is not stated.'

Murihiku: A History of the South Island of New Zealand and the Islands Adjacent and Lying to the South, from 1642 to 1835, Robert McNab

For Rosa

The stories we tell are always about ourselves.

The Talmud

CHAPTER 1

The Hunt

The Tasman Sea, 1805

'This is the hunting ground boys, here.' Captain Evans' stubby forefinger tapped at some dots on a map. McIntyre tilted his head, wondering how much land we were looking at.

'We will hunt along this chain, an island every month or so. Then all the way round the larger island to the west. Then home boys, full to the brim.'

The image of the mainland looked like a jagged potato. The larger island to the south was shaped like a pear.

'That island there, how far is it?' asked Scottish Jack.

'That's the mainland there, so it's that far,' insisted the captain. 'We'll just cut through the strait, head south.'

'Begging your pardon captain,' said McIntyre, 'but where did you get this map from?'

'Never flaming mind where I got it from, it's where we're going.'

The captain took another sip of his rum. I had seen maps and charts, newly made, in the governor's tent at the cove, in the hand of Lieutenant Dawes on the *Supply*. They were delicate things, the lines of ink as fine as hair, the coastline flowing like a riverbank, the land shaded a faint rose. This one looked like it had been fashioned by a child, the child being Evan Evans, captain of the *Speedwell*, our patched up, shrunken schooner. A squat Welshman, he was the only one of us comfortable in a cabin. He was bullish and ill-tempered; his voice hoarse from years of shouting into the wind. By then he was too fond of the rum to run a ship and we were always an unsteady vessel, from the moment we set sail. He put his glass down on the edge of the map.

'This island here is where you'll start right. I'd say there'll be a good ten mile of seals laying on a plate for you.'

'Aye and there might be some Maori warriors too, who for some strange reason think that the seals belong to them,' said Scottish Jack.

'It's the end of the earth. There's no-one there, seals and birds that's all.'

'You think my people are savages, but they know how to make boats. And that stretch of water … you're sure it's there?'

Scottish Jack had said his piece, leaving the captain no choice.

'I know it to be there even if you don't, because one of *my* people has been through it. We go where I say we go. The owner pays me to get him skins and that's where they are. You don't want to go? I'll drop you off first landfall. You can go back to your own people, whoever they imagine they are.'

Scottish Jack was the son of a whaler and a Maori woman. Her Maori man had been killed and Scottish Jack, as his mother called him, had Maori brothers, knew the language and the ways, but he chose to go sealing with white men. I had been hunting with him before, around Van Diemen's Land, but the waters there were bleeding dry. The captain shifted his stare back to the map.

'I'll head west to these islands, come back to pick you up with a pile of skins. Then we all work the main island.'

'How long captain will we be on the rocks for?'

'A month at a time. But you know the way it works Ruse. It's not the weeks or the days, it's the skins. If you don't have enough skins when I come back, and there's seals sat around, we all stay put until we do.'

'We could do with a fourth man,' I ventured.

'Why?'

'We could work in pairs, a rookery a piece. Still leaves you with five.'

'Oh right, and one of them's a cabin boy.' He put his hand to his brow. 'Take Williams then.'

'Christ,' said McIntyre, taking his pipe out of his mouth, 'a few months sleeping in a cave with him, seals might not be the only thing I'm skinning.'

The captain's eyes were off the map and on us.

'You'll have a lifeboat and a rifle. But don't shoot a seal or go anywhere until I find you, understood?'

With that, he rubbed his eyes with the heel of his hands, his cabin a haze of smoke and liquor. McIntyre released his pipe again.

'Captain, do you mind if I ask a question, about the money here?'

'The money was agreed before any of you set foot aboard.'

'Aye I know, but a question has occurred to me. You see, tragic as it is, men tend to die on voyages like this. And I was wondering, in that event, what happens to the man's take?'

'It goes to his family, always does.'

'Aye, but we being who we are, some of us don't have families. Are we going to send Williams' take back to some whorehouse in London? Because he has no-one, and I have no-one, and will say here and now, if I fall one dark night and drown, youse can have my lay. I'd rather it went to you than the owner. Wouldn't you say?'

Scottish Jack nodded twice. 'He has a point, otherwise we're just skinning day and night for the owner's pocket.'

Evans poured himself another drink.

'No-one is going to die on this voyage. Now, be gone.'

It had been almost a week since we'd sailed between the heads of Sydney Harbour. Some days we made good time, others we heeled and floundered in heavy water, for the sea and the skies changed temper so quickly, telling us one thing then another. Humpbacks were on our path heading south to breed, a whaler following their tails a day behind. It was a vessel twice our size, its men clothed in the skins we had come to tear from seals. We were beyond what I had believed some fifteen years before to be the very edge of the world, and that morning, when I saw Evans' map, I feared we were lost to man and God. A fog had us buried, muffling wind and sea, all I could hear was the creaking of rope and timber. My friend, John Williams was tightening the staysail. McIntyre brushed passed him, snarling something, pointing in my direction. Williams didn't reply and I expect didn't understand. I went to explain.

'How are you John?'

'I'm alright.'

'Funny name this boat has, don't you think?' I said.

His face was frozen, shut to most feeling, as it had been this past year, had been I reckoned since we first met. A moment or two later he said, 'Boats are as fast as the wind is, or the oarsman.'

She'd run aground in Broken Bay, was salvaged and rebuilt on the Hawkesbury by a man I know, had known since we were both convicts. When the floods washed the farmers out, he put me and others on his boats sealing for him. Men have been killing seals on the shores of New South Wales for the last ten years; it is empty of them. Then Van Diemen's Land, now we go further still, too far it seems. And McIntyre was right, men do die. They are capsized overboard, or they slip on the rocks in the dark, or their boats don't come back for them. He once told me a story about four men, who were left on an island, and their boat never came back for them, for it had sunk. Marooned they were, for four years, eating seal, wearing the skins, drinking the blood and the brackish water. He told me when they were rescued, though none were more than twenty-five years of age, they bore the appearance of ancient people. Then there will always be men who like to kill other men. Scottish Jack apart, the *Speedwell* was crewed by former convicts, from the captain to the cabin boy; people who needed quick money, who had failed at other ways; who would take risks and shed blood for coin and for vengeance.

Williams threw out his arm, pointing. 'At least she knows where she's going.' The fog had burned away and we could see in the distance on one side a broken headland, white peaks above, holding up one long feather of a cloud. On the other side, much lower land, glowing green. A current took us on its back and before our bows the wings of a whale rose from the sea, came crashing down, throwing spray onto the deck, waving us onward. We surged through the swell, through the great cleft in the land as if following behind Moses, until we came to our island where lilac water waited, calm and oily. We had come to the islands of New Zealand, and its beauty came upon me as Zion, as out of some dream, just as the days around me seem now, and all my days before, rolling back and forth through my mind, like surf to a shore.

CHAPTER 2

Snared

South Petherwin, Cornwall, 1782

The evening gorse gave off the smell of a baby's skin. For the first time in a while I had thought of our first born, baby Elizabeth, and for a moment, I was glad. I was carrying three rabbits to a new stone house outside the village, hidden down a clough, behind a line of beech. A pretty spot I'd always thought, and my eyes fell on an armful of firewood that I would glean later. I knew the young mistress there, Molly. We'd played together as children and walked out together when we came of age. But now she was married to Thomas Olive, an older man, a man too busy to catch his own rabbits. I would only get sixpence for the three, but one was little more than a kit, and had stood staring blindly inside my trap before I tugged the noose and choked it.

A way before the back door I could smell the juices of a meat cooking in the breeze; my stomach moaned. Molly let me in the back door and hung the rabbits over the hearth. In the corner, a cat lay with a mouse between its teeth. Molly had filled out to womanhood but I could still see the girl I once knew.

'Good mouser?' I asked.

'The best. He's getting on, but he's sly.'

'I'll skin those rabbits for you, if you want.'

She looked unsure, her brown eyes far away. Then she smiled and took a knife from the drawer.

Although I didn't ask, I could tell the master wasn't in the house. I set about my work on the table, pulling each skin off whole like a glove whilst she stood close to me.

'Your master treating you all right is he?'

'He's not my master, he's my husband.'

'Oh,' I said, 'so you don't do whatever he asks then?'

'No I don't. What about your Susanna then, she keeping well?' Her voice was restful and young.

'She's tired. Been working all day. Unlike some I know.'

She stepped away from me and tended to a pot on the hearth. Mutton with so much thyme I could feel it on my tongue. Around the kitchen, there was a bacon hanging, bowls of gooseberries, eggs, a pie. It was a few weeks larder and I drank in the sight of it.

'Plenty of food here, don't know why you need these rabbits.'

'Squire's coming to dinner. You seen his appetite?' she asked.

'I've seen the upshot.'

'Well it's not as big as his wife's.'

I'd scared crows from her father's field for tuppence a day from when I was seven. Her mother died a few years later and her father, a stupid man, swung a scythe against his own ankle which took bad until he became lame and useless. She married a man from Bristol five minutes after he came galloping into the village, and he paid to have the house built. He was older than her by some ten years, but no older than my Susanna was to me.

Molly opened the back door to let out the fog from the stove. She stood on the threshold, hands on hips, her back to me. I put down my knife and wiped my hands on my shirt. I took a step towards her and reached a hand for her waist but just as I closed in, she stepped forward and bent down to pick something. She straightened, surprised to find me so near.

'Want to take some lavender home?' she asked, 'I've plenty. Calm you down, James.'

'We have some. So, friends with Squire Tredwen are yer?' I said.

'Thomas wants to buy some more fields.'

'More common land is it?'

Her bearing changed with the question.

'I'll go get your sixpence then.'

Thomas Olive had already taken a swathe of commons pasture, we'd petitioned against it but it was all a waste of ink. Now he was after more. I heard Molly's footsteps on the stairs. Who has to go upstairs for a sixpence? The cat licked its paws. I looked at the backdoor; a makeshift job with daylight between two panels. I leaned in to the latch and lifted it like a leaf. I laid it back down softly as a baby's head and poked my skinning knife inside the crack. Molly's footsteps were in the hallway. She slipped into the kitchen and held out my sixpence like a prize. When I took it there was a stroke on my hand, I was sure of it.

'You want me to bring you a brace next week?' I asked.

'If you like then.'

Outside I held the sixpence up to the curdling light. It looked well-made, but too tarnished at the edges, and beaming at the centre. I figured the weight of it on my finger. I was about to pick-up the firewood when I saw, on the hill above, Olive's shepherd looking down, watching me. Like most labourers he'd need any favour he could get from a master, so I left it where it lay. It was still July but the light was mellowing like August; autumn was to come early that year. I came off his land and by the village pasture my two cows were chewing on bird's-foot and clover; soon his sheep would be herded-in and the field nibbled down to the earth. Only one of my cows had calved that year, like the other knew someone was coming for the grass. When I'd played scarecrow for Molly's father, the village pasture ran all the way to the river, not even the Tamar was ours' no more. Swallows were out hunting, diving in long loops, in another hour it would be the bats, then the owls out hunting for them. I cut off the track through a hedge. I stepped over some yarrow, the very place I'd picked it the year before for Susanna to make something to try and save Elizabeth with. I headed down the side of the squire's field. It was my strip once, my barley strip and I made a point of walking straight through his crop, since all the grain would go to Launceston and it would be lucky if he hired me to load his cart. It's yet to happen.

Susanna was sitting on a stool outside our cottage. She leaned back against the wall, guarding her eyes from the sunset. I tossed her the sixpence, she studied it, pressed it between her teeth. My boy Richard chased one of our chickens across the track.

'Not bad, seen worse.'

'Think you can spend it?' I asked.

'Oh I'll spend it. In the market. On a busy day.'

We went inside for our own dinner. A rabbit for the three of us that would have to last for a few days. Susanna knew how to stew and spice game. She kept our cottage, sewed my clothes, and made whatever baby Richard required. I was only nineteen when I met and married her, she, thirty-three. Four years on and she'd been bringing in hay from first light. She handed me my stew and stumbled into the hearth burning her hand.

'Did he take on any men with you today?' I asked her.

'No. And you asked me that yesterday, just me and a boy. You know what he said? He said with the rent being what it is, the best they can hope for is a war. Puts up the price of food he says.'

Her eyes fell shut before her plate was empty. I put Richard to bed. He would fight his sleep since I had got him up the last few nights, to show him the deer that came to the meadow behind us. A roe fawn, standing stone still in the grass, its coat the colour of seed heads. I watched Susanna sleeping in the chair while I thought about Molly and her husband, her master, Thomas Olive. Few I knew would have said a good word about him, but all slight was spoken away from earshot. He was barrel-wide, fierce in expression, had been a navy man in Newfoundland where he claimed to have 'chopped-up savages'. He came to Petherwin from Bristol, came with money, more than the Admiralty paid. There was talk that he had come with coins made by himself and his associates. For sure, the man was a faker of the king's shilling and not always careful with it. Yet there were as many clipped coins around as minted and nobody minded. People said the squire had paid labourers with them. I wondered how Olive was with Molly, imagined them together, his body writhing across hers' like a lizard. Susanna woke and hobbled to our bed with her eyes shut. She slept in her clothes whilst I looked at the night sky. It was as if she could feel the clouds move across the moon, for just before I rose she muttered to me, 'Be careful James,' her hand clenching my shirt.

So I returned to their house but through the village first. As I hoped, I saw Thomas Olive drinking outside a public house, prattling to a group of men. I headed the other way, past one of the Davies boys, thrashing birds from the hedge. I told him to be in his bed and he shouted curses back at me. I eased down into the clough, couldn't see my hand in front of my face. I heard movement I'm sure, two twigs snapping and stopped still for a moment. A poacher perhaps? I sat and watched Molly's candlelight in the upstairs window. She was saying her prayers or writing a letter to her thickerd father. The white throat of a fox flashed-up at me then the light from its eyes was gone. Molly's window went black and I lay on my back. There are sailors who can tell wherever they are in the world by looking at stars. The heavens are a map on a table, turned upside down.

I slid down from between the trees to the path and took off my boots. I got to the back door, took out the skinning knife and eased it into the crack. I brought it up slowly, lifting the catch with my ear to the door. I edged it open and was in the kitchen with the cold silence of stone under my feet. There was nothing there for me. In the parlour next door I found a dresser and a coffer. The top drawer had cutlery and I pocketed some. The middle drawer some linen and the bottom drawer inside a cloth were two watches, silver. Starling's eggs in a nest. I snatched at them and headed for the back door knowing Susanna and I were set, I had in my pocket a few months of rent on a farm of our own. I had a means to feed my family, so that my son would not perish like his sister had.

I opened the door and a flintlock was pushed in my face, the barrel beneath my eye. Thomas Olive's right hand held the other end, his left outstretched for his watches. Behind me Molly's voice said, 'Better give me that knife, James Ruse.'

I handed it over without turning round. Thomas Olive's face was like a fist. Like a dog's face before a fight, tightened from the inside.

'Fetch a stool for him Molly,' his eyes fixed on mine.

He sat me in the middle of the kitchen, his stare didn't stray as he took a step back to kick my shins, hard as he could, time-after-time, until he needed to get a breath. I didn't make a sound. He told Molly who was behind me to leave and she obeyed him. He held out one of the watches before me.

'You'll swing for this,' he said.

'You'll swing for clipping coins.'

Molly was back standing at the open door. I looked straight at her.

'Out!' he yelled at her.

She jumped back and went away and I was too frightened to look at him. He spoke to me quietly, like he was talking to a child.

'We caught some savages in Canada. We had quite a time with them. I put a musket barrel up against a brave's eye and pulled the trigger. He rocked back, fell on his arse and then stood up again, with his chest out for what must have been a minute before he dropped down dead. I've never known how. Stand up boy.'

I didn't move, I couldn't look at him. He dipped down to find my eyes and I saw the barrel approach one of them until he pushed hard on it, my head was forced back as far as my neck would allow.

'Stand up.'

I got-up, my leg twitching, the piss running out of me. He stood back and laughed.

'That's what you'll do when you're kicking at the end of a rope,' he declared, and pitched me out the house.

CHAPTER 3

Seized

I ran home like a scolded boy caught stealing apples, except then I knew there would be a future when it wouldn't matter, when it was only a memory. I slid into bed next to Susanna, she rubbed her feet against mine, I rubbed mine back, then turned away and wept as quietly as a man is able to.

In the morning, she was dressing Richard whilst I was still in bed.

'What did you get?' she asked.

'Couple of spoons.'

She polished one on her apron, squinted at the hallmark.

'Is that all? No coin then?'

'He keeps it upstairs.'

'Can't rent no land on what we'll get for these.'

Her face was fixed with suspicion. I went to fill the pails without a word. The night had been chilly but the day was warm though the sun wasn't in the sky, left blank silver grey. I waited at the pump whilst women talked ahead of me. One of them, the priest's maid, asked how Richard was doing and, though I never said a word to her, began to talk about the shame of losing Elizabeth at three weeks, telling me how we should be thankful she was baptised in time. I looked past her at the priest in his porch, behind a foot of grass, robed and ready to greet people.

I filled both pails and hooked them with the pole across my back. As I crossed the lane the squire and his family came past, his boy no more than five, clad in stockings, velvet breeches, a hat too big for his head. His father gave me work and he gave others tenancies and I saluted him. Then before I was across the lane and on to our track, something splashed in one of the pails. I looked up and hail stung my face, falling like flint from above. I put down the water and looked at ice stones the size of acorns skipping around my feet, splashing away my water. The squire's family had run for the porch while he was catching them in his hands, examining them between his fingers til they melted. He looked at me and nodded to confirm the wonder. A moment later the hail stopped as suddenly as it began. I washed in one of the pails outside and shouted in at Susanna, 'Brush your hair, we're going to church.'

She came outside, her hands and face black from the hearth.

'We hardly ever go to church.'

'I know, but we're going today.'

She took the other pail round the side, took off her smock, and washed herself. She was talking half to herself, half to me, 'Labourers like us aren't seen in church … we don't have the clothes for a start.'

I went to her, her face flushed with water.

'We have a right in church as much as anyone,' I said.

'Are you sure James? What did you do last night? Have you forgotten the Commandments?'

I went over to her and lowered my voice.

'I know the Bible better than most. People who go to that church and line the front pews, they're the thieves. The squire taking common land for himself, eating with a coiner who has no end of money but doesn't work for it. The money I was after wasn't his, and I did it … I did it because our strip of land was taken and our pasture as well. We owe rent on our cottage, soon we'll be beggars on the road. Turfed out. And the squire and the coiner will be on the front pew the week after. That is the greater sin.'

'People like us James, they go to the chapel. That's where the poor will be.'

'Aye and they'll have to listen to my father. We'd be turfed out of there all right. We're going to the village church,' I snapped, 'get the boy.'

Susanna was more ashamed of who we were than what I'd done. The respectable of the parish looked their best for church on Sundays and did their worst for the poor the rest of the week. My father had turned to Methodism when I was a boy. He kept us out of the regular church and brought me to a Meeting House instead. I learned my letters through the Bible. He had me reciting psalms when I was waist high, had hopes of me ministering and so did I, but after I met Susanna, after I put her with child, I was out on my ear.

We got to church as the last bell was dying and stuck to the back wall by the mercy seats. The Davies boy had scrawled his name on the seat next to mine. A psalm was sung and at its end when people sat down I saw, on a front row pew, that gypsy-black hair tied up in a rat's tail. The faker of coins and murderer, piously looking up at the priest, Molly's head bowed beside him. The priest spoke the parable of the virgins, told us how we had to be prepared for bad harvests, for our judgement day and I could see the side of Thomas Olive's face, chin lifted, pretending to take it all in. I began to take it in myself. The foolish virgins, unprepared as I was. And those who had acknowledged God, who would not help the fools, fools like me. My insides quivered again and I was glad my stomach was empty for I dry-retched. The congregation turned and Richard began to cry. Susanna took him outside. I straightened myself and looked back at Molly and her master before pulling the door behind me.

'Is that what you did then, spend what you got at the tavern?'

'I told you, I didn't get any coin,' I said.

I was sat on the porch step leaning on the wall as if I had run a mile. Susanna was comforting Richard, half-crying herself.

'Something's turned your stomach.'

'It'll be because there's nothing in it.'

'We'll there'll only be one meal today.' Susanna lifted Richard to her breast and they left me. I should have gone and worked on the kitchen garden, but there was no purpose inside me. I walked behind the church and onto the squire's land, across two farms and into the meadows that no-one had cut for hay or ploughed for seed since three years.

There was, some way into the meadows, half-covered in moss and grass and fern, a ruin; three sides and no roof, more than we needed for the bones of a cottage. I stepped inside and turned in a circle. I could see a room with a floor, with furniture, a coffer of our own, a mirror, pots, hanging from the beam. Susanna was upstairs where we slept, Richard outside with his pup, for we could feed a dog now as well as ourselves. I was standing in a tomorrow that I knew I could only dream of. My only hope at that moment was that I was right about Thomas Olive being a coiner. Someone was clipping coins and, if it was him, he might be wary of standing in court to accuse me of stealing watches.

I lay on my back until the dread of the night before had left me, so I was not so overcome I couldn't think clearly. I decided I would tell Susanna that I had been caught and that she had to be prepared, that I could not prepare myself without her. Two jackdaws were squabbling over the guts of a small bird on the gable end, then at once scuttling about my face and ankles were two spaniels.

'Ruse. Here again,' came the squire's voice like a major.

I got to my feet and stood to attention.

'I'm sorry for the trespass sir, I only wanted to look at the ruin and the meadows. I had heard there might be a tenancy going here.'

He was about to say something but I kept going, talking ever faster.

'I know my crops and my livestock, I rotated my strip, and this would make a good home for my family. I reckon I could make these fields work.'

He walked over to one of the broken walls, rested his palm on a block of stone.

'A gamekeeper lived here.' He looked back at me, sensing my question. 'They went, moved on, Camelford, maybe.'

I didn't ask why because I knew he would've been the cause of it. And then like a confessor he told me.

'These won't be meadows much longer. I'll be wintering sheep here. The stone what's left will be used to make a wall. There's more money in sheep than tenants, and less bother. It's not what I want but it is a fact. Best be off home.'

I couldn't go home lugging more bad news, so I went to the vicarage and asked if I could cut the graveyard grass for sixpence. Still chewing his dinner, Father Silva walked me through his walled garden, ample with fruit, pointing to a scythe and rake.

'Come see me after you've finished,' he said with his back turned.

I sharpened my blade and began at my mother's grave. Elizabeth Ruse. She died not long after my brother Issac was born. I was seven and I can't remember my father speaking to me until years later, except sometimes he would say a prayer whilst we were in the fields. I got into an easy swing and, though my head was light, I had scythed and gathered it all up within the hour. I went to his door and asked if I could take the hay off in sacks for my manure pit. He bid me into the kitchen and asked me to sit. He passed a sixpence across the table and showed me some lambs' tails on a piece of cloth.

'You'll be hungry by now I expect?'

He folded it and I had my hand on it before I thanked him.

'I'm sorry we had to walk out this morning, it was my stomach playing up,' I said.

'We'll that should help you then.'

Father Silva's face was gnarly, his nose bubbling, but his eyes kindly.

'There is a psalm I used to know. My mother knew it by heart and would ...'

'I remember your mother,' he said to me, 'and I remember the psalm she loved.'

'*For the godly man ceaseth ...*' the rest of the line forgotten to me.

He raised a finger then left the room returning with two Bibles.

'Psalm Twelve it is. Shall we try it James, a verse each?' He began, '*Help me Lord for the godly man ceaseth, for the faithful fail from among the children of men,*' and the words came to me, without the book.

'*They speak vanity every one with his neighbour, with flattering lips and with a double heart do they speak.*'

We spoke in step, spoke it like a catechism.

'*The Lord shall cut-off all flattering lips, and the tongue that speaketh proud things.*'

'*Who have said, with our tongue will we prevail, our lips are our own: who is lord over us?*'

'*For the oppression of the poor, for the sighing of the needy, now will I arise, saith the Lord. I will set him in safety from him that puffeth at him.*'

'*The words of the Lord are pure words: as silver tried in a furnace of earth, purified seven times.*'

'*Thou shalt keep them, O Lord, thou shalt preserve them from this generation for ever.*'

'*The wicked walk on every side, when the vilest men are exalted.*'

We closed our books as one.

'James, your mother watches down on you. If you are ever in such need again, she would tell you to come to this house.'

'I shall. Father, I have something else to ask. There is a verse my father used to quote, Leviticus.'

I went straight to the chapter, the verse, put my finger on it, and showed it to him while I recited, *And when ye reap the harvest of your land, thou shalt not make clean riddance of the corners of thy field when you reapest, thou shalt leave them unto the poor.*'

'See father it is our right to glean the field after harvest. That's what is said in the Bible, yet there are people in the pews who wouldn't let us glean last harvest.'

'And you'd like me to read this in a sermon before the coming harvest?' he asked.

I nodded, like a Sunday school child.

'James there is the law of God and then there are the laws of men, and they are not the same.'

He rose to his feet and I left, tossing the two laws around in my mind, a ripened apple from hand-to-hand. I topped-up my haysack with wood on the way back and with the lambs' tails, it all cheered Susanna. She was working on the kitchen garden and we had onions and leeks fried with our meat. I felt obliged to say grace at the table then she laughed, couldn't stop herself, Richard copying as well.

'What's so funny then?'

'I buried the spoons. Not worth the risk selling them or keeping them … maybe some more'll grow.'

I couldn't talk about the night before, what could await me. If destruction was on its way let it come. I realised I had never tired of looking at her face. A face beautiful in its strength. I let the talk run where she wanted it to go. She talked about one day sending Richard to school, she'd had so little education herself. Neither could I tell her that the squire was putting his sheep on the meadows I had in mind for a farm. Year by year it was getting harder for labourers to advance to farmers, or to live from their labour. Land fell into fewer hands and people were driven away like crows after ploughing. She wanted to know where we would look for work the coming week, surely there was plenty to be had; hay taken in and covered, hoeing, ditches dug again, fruit picked, willow and hazel cut for fences. We thought we would work hard and eat well for the next month. When it came to it that week we were always *too late* or *just unlucky I'm afraid.* By the Thursday, we were walking to Lawhitton and then Launceston, carrying Richard all the way, then in the field all day digging onions. Sometimes the sight of an infant can put farmers off hiring, sometimes it helps. I knew why there was no work for either of us in Petherwin, Susanna I think was frightened to ask. Thomas Olive had put it about, had given instructions to those he could, to refuse us work. The squire had the land and the coiner had the people, all in their pockets. I wondered at the charity of Father Silva, about where that would go when he knew of my stealing. We were a marked family. Another week or two of this and we would be on the parish. The idea came to me that the next day we should walk as far west as we could, where I would try for the mines. As we finally came along the lane to the turn of our track, Susanna shouted to me, 'James, what's that here for?'

Ahead of us was a lock-up waggon, coffin black. I stopped dead and stared at the chamber, the iron door, and its barred window. I should have run. Run straight south and worked my passage on any ship going anywhere. A sheriff walked out from behind the waggon, next to him a boy holding irons. I'd never seen this man before but his reputation was known to me. He was a sallow looking individual as was the boy. The man's naked arms were not wide but looked strong as axe handles. His neck was lean and all veins; hanging off his belt was a dagger for stabbing and a cudgel that could crack limbs. The boy's eyes were on me like prey. He was leaning forward, ready to move. Somehow the sheriff's dog had got behind us and was snarling at Susanna. The sheriff opened the door on the waggon and looked my way. He did not approach me, it was as if I was already his prisoner.

'James Ruse I have a warrant to take you to a magistrate in Bodmin.'

I looked round at his dog, short legs, panting at not having to move. I'd outrun it and him. The boy would be fast. Susanna with Richard asleep in her arms moved between me and the sheriff.

'On what charge is it?' she asked.

'He stole two watches, silver,' shouted the boy.

The sheriff looked angrily at his charge. Susanna began cursing and yelling full pelt at them. I looked out to the field to my left. I'd have to fight my way through a summer hedge but by the time the sheriff had done the same I'd be into the woods. The boy I would wallop. He must have read me, must have seen a number run, for he pushed his dagger into Susanna's cheek and told me, 'You don't get in this waggon and I'll peel a piece off her face to feed my dog.'

He was ready to carve into her cheek and yet I couldn't walk to the cage, no more than a beast willingly walks to slaughter, its eyes washed with mortal knowledge. The instant I raised a foot off the ground the sheriff's boy ran to meet me and closed an iron shackle round my wrist. I held out my other arm for him and the sheriff sheathed his dagger. They pulled me by the chain into the waggon without a word. And I spoke not a word, gave not a look to Susanna.

CHAPTER 4

My Dungeon

The sheriff and his boy spoke not a word to me on the way to Bodmin. It is the way of gaolers. A guard will no more offer conversation to a prisoner than a butcher to a carcass. The door bolt clanked on a dungeon, a pit, and James Ruse began to die. I had thought once that he had only begun to sleep, to hide until he could lock his own door, but I know now that the man I had been was buried alive. I sat on a stool listening to the drip of water, counting the seconds between each tiny splash. I thought about Paul in his prison in the Bible. He sang hymns when they put his feet in the stocks and God sent an earthquake to free him, the gaoler on his knees and asking for forgiveness, *what must I do to be saved?* I listened to people tell the story like they had seen it happen. That was in the Meeting House, before the chapel was built and I was a boy, nine at most, in wonder at the scripture then, but when my dungeon finally came I was without the heart to sing.

They had been waiting for me, Thomas Olive and Molly. They had read me without me knowing. All most of us have time to think about is the next meal. But some, who don't have to worry about that, they are thinking of the years to come, even the years after they have gone. I wondered that night, as I do now, how little time I had left. Only now I am not filled with the fear I was then.

The next morning the sheriff opened the door and, before I could stand, his boy put irons around my ankles to match my wrists. He stepped away from me.

'On your feet,' he scowled.

The weight of the chain and bracelets had me walking like my grandmother did once, four steps for everyone elses's one. We went from the bridewell to the street and I was beset by light and noise of carts and horses, of children and hawkers. The sheriff held a cudgel and looked about him as if expecting someone to attempt my rescue, but I was no highwayman, no Jacobite. We reached the gaol and I was taken into the gatehouse and told to stand facing the wall. A man came into the room and the sheriff left. I looked behind and watched him put an inkwell and quill, paper and chalk on the table. His eyes reached up towards mine but he disregarded me, his drawn face stamped upon as any labourer's.

'What will happen to me?' I asked.

He scratched with the quill, looking only at his paper. A moment later, he stood to attention for what reason I did not know. He must have had ears like a bat for there was some lull before the door opened. A man came in with the height of a child and the face of a hag. He looked on my ungodly sight, taking from his pocket a handkerchief to hold to his nose. He pointed for me to sit in the chair, took out his rum flask for a sip.

'A charge has been laid against you. Do you know what it is?'

I shook my head.

'Burglary,' he said.

'Oh,' I said.

'Are you thirsty?'

'Aye,' I said.

'Clerk, fetch him some small beer and some for me. This on Friday last. How do you plead?'

I was struck dumb. He fetched some wax out of one of his ears, flicked it away and said, 'I should say if you plead guilty you'll be hanged without a trial. The charge is that you burglariously broke and entered the dwelling-house of Thomas Olive stealing two silver watches.'

'Well I'm not guilty,' I replied.

He wrote it all down and the beer arrived, we said nothing but drank instead.

'Where were you then, that night?' he asked.

I took another drink.

'I need to do the necessary,' I told him.

The frown on the clerk's face which was itself all of a frown grew, and he hauled me by my wrist-chain to the privy. I had to think my answer through. If I named Susanna she would be questioned and if found lying, sent to gaol which would be the death of Richard. If I said I went to the house to be a cuckolder with Molly, and we'd been caught by her master, Susanna would be shamed, Molly deny it all the same.

'Well,' asked the magistrate, 'where were you?'

'I was at bed. Next to my wife all night. As I have been every night for the last three years now.'

The clerk scratched it all down and the sheriff led me into the gaol, took off my irons, and put me in a cell, twice the size of the bridewell. In the darkness of a corner I could see a boy with his knees up to his chest, the light from his bones glowing beneath his skin. After first glance, he would not look at me because he feared me. Between the dirt, his flesh bore the paleness of a fish.

'What's your name boy?'

'I'm called George.'

'Same as the king, eh?'

'I wouldn't know about that.'

There was, from another cell, the cries of a woman off her hooks, pleading for mercy, pleading her innocence, then pleading to be hanged. *'I haven't done anything no I haven't done it... but send me from here and hang me and damn me will you...'*

'How old are you George?'

'Nine maybe.'

'Been stealing apples have you?'

'No.'

'Where's my girl... where's my girl where's she gone where have you taken her... don't give her to those men don't do that. Those men, those men darling darling are you all right? Are you? Don't cry, don't cry, I'm here, I'm here, I am... mother's here.'

'I stole a pair of stockings. They say.'

'They say?'

The boy stood and I saw the height of him, the frame of him, under the rags hanging on him.

'James Grace, he got me into this. He's a codshead he is, can't do a sneak without getting caught. Caught three times he has been.'

'I'll have to end you girl end you I shall … better than those men, those men, have you … don't no, no don't cry my child.'

'I said to him we should have washed the soot off us. Black our faces only, 'cept we left the soot behind on doors and windows.'

'Chimney sweep, are you?'

'Sometimes I have been.'

I had seen sweeps about Launceston, Bodmin too, working in the town houses of merchants and squires. Urchins bandy and black from head to shoeless feet. Sweeps were flushed-out of chimneys with fire falling from height to break on the ground, and dug out of them dead sometimes. Come the last fires of May, they were left to filch for themselves. George would have no father or mother I knew, and more than likely would have been here since the summer began. I took it that he had had company in the cell leaving him fearing men. We were given pease and bread, he rushed to his food and gobbled it with his back to me, looking over his shoulder like a chary creature. I spoke to him about my life, about farming, about how you learn when to cut hay or harvest wheat to the exact day, right up to the rain, breathing the dampness in through your nose. How my father taught me to scythe. I lied to the boy, saying I had my own farm.

'Thirty acres. Know what an acre is? About as far as you could run full pelt. I got mostly sheep, some barley. Soil's not bad for Cornwall.'

I spoke like I expected to be farming the next day, there being no use telling him since he would never work the land, even if either of us were to see it in daylight or darkness again. All night I heard the woman's crazed cries until they stopped dead half way through a word.

CHAPTER 5

The Island

We pushed off from the *Speedwell* with a canvas, nets, water barrel, a rifle, and clubs. Evans had anchored some way out, for there were sandbanks all about and, if she ran aground, all would be lost. He had put me in charge of the other three and said he'd return in a month. I watched him weigh anchor and chase the wind taking him west. The water was still and over the shallows it had the colour of whey. The sky too was pale liquid, the murk of the day before, vanished. Our island had wavy hills, dunes, and a stream cutting into the beach. The sand was butter and all across the beach, what from a distance looked like rocks, were seals, waiting to be slaughtered for their skins. We dragged our boat through them, the bulls snarling, the pups waddling to the side. We staked out our canvas between the dunes and went looking for firewood. There wasn't much. Some hunched trees, pieces of driftwood; it was going to be a cold month.

'We may as well get on with it,' I said to them.

'You don't think we should scout the island first?' suggested Scottish Jack.

'For what?' asked McIntyre. 'You think anyone could live here? There's no-one here but us.'

Sealers had been killed by Jack's people on the mainland. New Zealand natives are not like the natives of New Holland. They are fearsome warriors who were fighting the settlers on the mainland as soon as they set a foot down; it was why Evans had us plunder the small islands.

'Tomorrow we'll look at the island, but there's a good six hours of daylight with the seals under our nose. Get your clubs.'

As far as we could, we came up behind them to break their skulls. No seal is ever shot, putting a hole in the skin. Their eyesight is poor, their hearing better, but it isn't what you'd call hunting; sitting with a snare, one shot with a rifle, more the slaughter of the innocents, the doe-eyed pups, the weighty adults. Some would waggle themselves away to the water, but on a beach like that you could always work your way through enough to make your shoulders sore. We had our different ways of culling, of killing. John Williams would lash and lash, swinging fast in all directions, then I'd catch him stock still, staring out at the horizon, at nothing. With McIntyre, it was as if he had to make himself hate each animal, bringing down the club with great power and then gazing at his work, the bloodied creature, the brains and bones, before choosing where next to swing. For Scottish Jack and me, it was hitting nails into wood. Only for the first few blows were they alive to us. A seal is not a chicken or a fish, and I believe that every hunter of so large a being bleeds inside with the first cull. If not with the killing, with the tearing-off of their skins, ripping them open from the neck down, pushing in the knife, right around, peeling it off like a coat.

Sundown had a yellowness to it. We would have to move round the island, if not for the seals, for the firewood. Seal oil burns well, but you need a sizable fire under the blubber to get to it. Only McIntyre ate his seal cooked. The rest of us ate it raw with our hard biscuits. The remainder of the meat rotted in abundance. Evans would take some of the blubber, but not enough to make it worth his while, not enough to kill so many. And their skins, these would go to London or Paris, where it was a great deal warmer. There was a stench of blood off us, corpses all across the sand but, further down the beach, light was shining off the fur of pups.

'There's nowhere to run a line to, is there?' said McIntyre.

'We can drive the oars into the sand, use them,' replied Williams.

'Some Robinson Crusoe, your man,' shouted McIntyre, looking at me.

We drove the oars into the sand fifty yards or more apart, and ran a line from one to another, hanging the skins off them to dry. As we did, flies came down and filled the face of evening. The tide coming in had turned to blood.

'We should go out tonight. We'll get a good haul.'

'What's the rush, we'll be here a month,' argued McIntytre.

'I'm not sure the seals will be, they've plenty of places to go where they won't be slaughtered'.

From the *Speedwell* I had seen another island to the west, and the mainland to the north.

'We'll give it an hour at the most. Williams and me, we'll start from the far end of the rookery, you two this end. We'll meet in the middle.'

We waded across the sand, and all we had slain that afternoon, towards the shimmer of new skins. We were invisible to them. I made my way across the top of the rookery to the other side, expecting John Williams to be behind me. When I shouted back, 'Leave the younger pups,' I saw him culling on McIntyre's patch. I called to him, waving him forward, but he was slamming down his club either side, riotously. McIntyre too was shouting. He shoved Williams in the back, who only faltered for a moment. McIntyre put a hand on Williams' shoulder, and as Williams brought his club up he swung it so high it came over his back and hit McIntyre. It amused me, but he'd hit him so hard I heard it. McIntyre fell to his knees, holding his forehead. We took him back to the shelter, the fire we'd put out. He lay on his back, the blood still pouring out of him with the curses. Scottish Jack wiped McIntyre's head and told Williams to get some dry kelp. I lit the fire.

'I don't think it's as bad as it looks, but we'll know more when the bleeding stops,' said Scottish Jack.

I tried to comfort him saying, 'It's sure to stop bleeding in a while.'

'Aye, when there's no blood left inside of me.'

The kelp may have had some healing properties but it didn't soak up much blood.

'I'm going to have to stitch it,' announced Scottish Jack. 'And I can't wait until it's light, you'll have lost too much blood by then.'

McIntyre swept Scottish Jack's hand aside.

'This was no accident Ruse. There's going to have to be a reckoning for this, and there will be, you'll see.'

We didn't bring any medicine. There was a needle and thread for sewing cuts and gashes and clothes. Scottish Jack had some experience of this, but that didn't mean he had a light touch.

'Ruse, hold the skin together.'

I put my knee on McIntyre's chest whilst Scottish Jack dug through the skin, tying the gash from crown to eyebrow. Williams looked on closely and silently for a while, then he turned his gaze out to the sea.

CHAPTER 6

Judgement

Bodmin Assizes

George and me were taken into a yard, there were two other prisoners standing with a gaoler. Irons were put about our legs and a chain linked the four of us. The two other prisoners were a blond haired bull of a man and a long necked dandy in a blue coat. Beyond the gate, I could hear a gathering of people, like a market day. When we got through the gate a crowd pressed against us, some spitting, some landing blows. Soldiers fought them back. A gaoler led the way dragging the chain, behind him the big man, then the dandy, then George and me. A woman scratched at my face then made the act of choking with her tongue pushed out, before laughing. Another woman, sobbing, embraced the dandy before being dragged-off him. George, the boy, was in front of me and couldn't keep up, couldn't carry his chains, the barrel-chested man pulled him off his feet. I shouted for him to wait, a soldier dug a rifle butt into my ribs. In the time it took for us to walk across the square to the courthouse we could have walked quarter of a mile.

The courthouse reminded me of a chapel where we lined-up before a pulpit. We were stood behind a bar looking up at the clamour, the livid faces in the gallery. Crones, ladies, soldiers, ragamuffins, gents, jostling and jeering as if the gallows was below. Then I heard her voice call me like she was calling me through the woods to the house. Susanna was at the back of the gallery and, though I could only glimpse her face, the glow of her hair in the window-light heartened me, and my dread and her comfort passed between us. A line of gentlemen entered the room, smoking pipes, fingering watches. Then the clerk from the day before and the magistrate, though he had now a wig on and a powdered face such that he resembled a puppet. After them, the man that would be my judge whose face was likewise a mask.

The whole room began to quieten as the dandy was unchained and called to the stand. Puppet-face said *he befriended a widow, coaxed, and charmed his way into her home, her arms, her chamber.* The widow, *trusted him, gave him gifts from her inheritance,* then, *he took her jewellery and fled into the night.* The gallery listened to the tale, he looked for a dose of pity, of admiration from anyone, but there was none. A witness came and described his character as *cruel, ruthless, a rake.* The gallery jeered. The magistrate whispered to the judge, then shouted out, 'Silence! Call the witness for the defence.'

A woman took the stand, powdered and wigged, wafting a fan. She curtsied.

'You know this man?' the judge asked of her.

'For several years, your Lordship.'

'What have you to say about this matter?'

'Well sir, I know him to be a gentleman, kind to ladies of all ranks, and we are prone to give him gifts. I wouldn't be surprised if the lady gave him the jewellery.'

'Really? Have you ever given him anything?' asked the judge.

The gallery laughed and the judge smiled along with them.

'Once or twice I might,' she answered.

'But you are not the widow are you?' said the judge.

'Dismissed!' shouted the magistrate.

The jury huddled, one of them stood but before he could speak the judge slammed down his hammer and said, *Guilty.* The rake hung his head, hid his parson's features, knew his fate was sealed. Susanna was looking at me, but I did not know how to look back. If a gentleman was condemned so easily, what of the rest of us?

The big man was a free-trader, caught with a supply of brandy. The judge asked where the excise men were, the witnesses. They were not in court and the jury quickly proclaimed him, *Not Guilty.* The gallery cheered as few Cornish would call a free-trader a villain. This angered the judge who had other charges for the man, *impersonating a seaman to draw their wages.* There was a paymaster witness who talked of bruises and brawls, the jury huddled and the foreman said, *Guilty.* The boy took the stand, his head just above the box.

'How old are you?' asks the judge.

'Going on nine.'

'What business was you bred-up in?'

'None. Sometimes a sweep.'

The judge pulled out a nosegay, fearing the gaol fever, held it against his face for a moment.

'Have you any father or mother?'

'Dead.'

'How long ago?'

'I do not know sir.'

The magistrate read out the charge, *Feloniously breaking and entering, burglariously stealing three pairs of silk stockings, value twelve shillings.* The shopkeeper says he saw the boy but couldn't catch him, 'He left his soot prints in my shop and we hunted the street until we found him.'

The judge was agitated, he knew what the jury would say, and he knew that more than ten shillings was the price of a hanging. He tapped his fingers and would not look at the foreman. His raised his eyebrows at George.

'Tell me, where are the stockings now?'

Before the boy could form a reply, the judge looked to the jury.

'Does he have them? Was coin found on him?'

No-one knew.

'We will leave the burglary aside and find the boy guilty of breaking and entering only,' and he hammered his desk.

The boy limped down to the pew to wait for his sentence, I was ordered to take the stand.

'James Ruse, how will you be tried?'

'By God and my country,' I said.

'James Ruse, you are charged with burglariously breaking and entering the dwelling-house of Thomas Olive during the night and stealing thereout two silver watches value five pound. How do you plead?'

'I plead not guilty.'

The magistrate muttered to the judge who told the jury, 'Says he was in bed with his wife,' to which the gallery whistled and laughed.

'Call Thomas Olive.'

Thomas Olive looked-up to his worship like the most law-abiding man in Cornwall, when he should have been lined-up with us. He gave his account to the court of how he had served his majesty in Canada like he was a friend of the king, and as such possessed a pistol. He gave an account of the night, of how he had been told I was at his house. Mrs Olive was called and Molly said what passed and could not look at me as she did. Then the boy Davies was called. He said he thought to follow me down the clough between the trees, then crept away to fetch Olive from the tavern. It is plain that they knew all along, from when I brought the rabbits round, knew because Molly saw me lift the latch with the skinning knife, knew from all the times I came to see Molly through one excuse or another, that I was after something I shouldn't be, and should be snared for it.

The magistrate pointed for me to leave the stand, I went back to the pew, and the judge passed sentence on all of us.

'William Bryant, George Taylor, you are to be transported to one of His Majesty's settlements on the coast of Africa for the term of seven years ... Harold Tunstall, James Ruse, it falls on me to sentence you to the severest penalty a court such as this can issue. You will be taken from Bodmin Gaol to a place of execution, and there hanged by the neck until you are dead. May God have mercy on your souls.'

We were put in a cell together. That was for me easier, to be with another condemned. When he looked at me I wanted to embrace him.

'We will die together,' I said.

'We will die alone,' he replied.

I had never seen a hanging but I could remember once, as a boy, working with my father and other men clearing stones, how someone told us he had yesterday seen a man hanged in Exeter. He said that the rope had slipped up the back of his neck and the man had taken a full ten minutes to die. As he told us, the man twitched his legs with his hands behind his back with his tongue pushed out, at which my father shouted at him. My neck I thought was broad, and I would ask the hangman to tighten the rope. It is one thing to say that a man should die well but when it comes to the final day, to your last hours, it takes all you can summon not to wail like an infant. The terror deranged me. The rake lay facing the wall. I was twenty-three; I had thought I had time to make more mistakes. He looked more than ten years older with the face of someone whose family didn't need a thief for a father. The cell door was unlocked, I got on my feet to meet them. It was Susanna with my son Richard. She walked towards me and looked at me like a mother upon her son. A son who had already been punished and whose heart was broken. I embraced her as a boy, *I am sorry, sorry ... I am leaving you both ... I should have seen this, Richard ... what will become of Richard?*

'I'll ask mother to take care of us. We shan't be on the parish.'

She put Richard in my unchained arms. My state disturbed him.

'I don't want you to come,' I said.

'I should be there, but I won't bring Richard.'

'Please,' I said to her. 'I can't say I'll be hardy at the end.'

She wasn't sure how to comfort me. Just her standing there with me, holding Richard, gave me strength. We spoke, but our words could not match the occasion. The gaoler was back in little time. Richard turned his face into his mother's breast as the gaoler led them away for good. The rake spoke to me from his corner, 'You think it is harder to leave them behind. To face death with them still living? I say it is harder to die in the knowledge that there is nothing left behind, no-one to mourn after you have gone. I refused marriage, family, the responsibilities of my breeding. For what? The card table, the bawdy house, and the foreseeable adventures of robbery.'

The gaoler came for me after the morning light had thickened, picking out a blinking rat. A hand was placed on my shoulder; he lifted me by the arm and led me to a blinding yard. My knees buckled as he stood me against a wall. The magistrate was there and behind him the bloated figure of the squire.

'James Ruse, found guilty to be hanged, you are hereby reprieved to be transported to one of His Majesty's settlements on the coast of Africa for the term of seven years pursuant to the statutory warrant this day August nineteen, the year, seventeen-eighty-two. Squire here says you know husbandry, says you might be of more use in a colony than jigging at the end of a rope.'

CHAPTER 7

Belly of the Whale

Dunkirk Hulk, Devonport, Winter 1782

I was taken to Devonport with the free-trader Bryant, young George and two others, all of us chained together, two days in a cart. Whenever one of us needed to relieve ourselves all of us had to accompany. People in Plymouth had thrown dirt and stones at us as we rode through. I was bloodied by the onslaught. From Plymouth out to the port we stood in silence on the quay, faces to a foul wind, man chained to man, but I was at least standing beneath a sky. Behind me there were trees, above me gulls. The sky had been boiling all morning, a storm about to spark. Out on the water a mile away the hulk rested steady inside its own haze. The clouds behind it bruised and it became a coffin to me. Four oarsmen brought a boat around and steadied it beneath us. On board was a redcoat, a veteran whose fighting days were over. The turnkey removed the chain that linked us, our arms and legs remained in shackles.

'In the boat with you,' yelled the redcoat.

He was old, scarred, sick maybe. His eyes like pebbles. A few hundred yards from the hulk the sea turned black and the wind served up its stench such that our eyes burned. The oarsmen pulled their tunics up over their faces, the third convict retched. Bryant nodded to an oarsman, 'You row like a wench,' he said.

The marine kicked Bryant. I figured the nearer I was to him the more often I would be kicked. A mist came about us then rain but it did not break the painted surface of the water. I looked at George, his face was blank, hardened to stench maybe. As we got closer to the hulk we began to hear the shouting of its ghosts and the groaning of the ship. We were rowed round the towering cliff of the stern. The redcoat yelled up, 'Five to come on board!'

A gangplank was lowered and we staggered up and onto the deck where a small ferret-faced captain waited for us. He told us calmly to stand in a line. The dead-eyed redcoat handed him a paper from which he read out our names and sentences. Then he told us, 'This is the prison ship where you will be kept until you are transported to one of our Majesty's colonies beyond the seas. If you behave well you will be unchained. If you brawl or steal from other convicts you will be flogged and shackled. Do what you can to avoid the fever.'

He walked away from us smartly before we were doused in sea-water from pumps and then taken to the decks below. Shivering though I was in wind and in rain, I would have stood day and night outside to where I was headed. There were two decks beneath and we were taken to the lower one. At first there seemed no light at all. I was conscious only of the curses and cries of half-men, the reek of the ballast churning in the belly of the ship. Then my eyes grasped great lumps, boulders shambling with chains. Cracks of light breaking through the barred portholes. I was in a cave of wood and iron. The redcoat from the quay unlocked a barred gate and pushed us into a cage that ran one side of the whole deck. On the other side; a similar cage. A half whispered voice called out to George, 'Boy... boy. Come over here. Got something nice for you to eat.'

A turnkey approached and removed my leg and arm chains. He wore a black uniform and a hat but was as miserable as any convict. He unchained the five of us and then he gave us all some clothing and some bread and cheese.

'This is your mess here. You get food for the mess, sleep in hammocks you scrub every two days,' he said hoarsely.

He had a squint in both eyes and after we had devoured the black bread and cheese, he came back with blankets and wrist chains. We were to be chained all the time it seemed, the weight of the irons on George hunching him and bleeding his arms. Soon they would go bad. Shackling a man for years kills him in the end. He will die from low spirits, be ready to be put into the earth before his body gives up. The four of us went to the benches at our mess. We had a porthole beside us facing out to sea;

our only blessing. Bryant sized up everyone around him. The redcoat patrolled the passageway down the middle of the deck tapping a drawn cutlass against his thigh as he walked.

'Some of us are in chains and some of us ain't. Notice that?' said Bryant.

Older, weaker men, some lying on their backs were chained; younger stronger men were not. I looked at the other man in our mess and I took his swarthiness, his hair and his eyes to make him an Irishman. His name was James Martin and he had stolen lead from a roof where he worked as a gardener.

'I was sure I was to be turned-off since the man I worked for was well acquainted with magistrates and judges.'

I told them that I owed my life to a squire.

'He petitioned the judge for me,' I said.

At which Bryant said that we had nothing to thank squires or the gentry or any Lords for, that it was time that people in England did what the people in America were doing: rising up against taxation and the Crown. Then Martin spoke-up as well.

'If they'd send me to America, I'd join the rebels.'

'I've been sentenced to transportation to Africa,' I said, 'all because of your revolution in America.'

'I heard off a seaman,' said Bryant, 'no-one lasts more than a couple of weeks out there. Diseases.'

'One thing's for sure,' came back Martin, 'we won't last long in here on this food.'

The redcoat must have heard Martin, for he unlocked the gate and came over to our mess. He was the kind of man, and I have known many of them, that takes pleasure from being another man's master. First out of his mouth, 'On your feet when you're in front of me.'

He had two stripes on his tunic and a scar on his forehead as wide as his mouth, which probably paid for the stripes. His eyes, even in the darkness, were button small.

'What's your name?'

'Bryant.'

'You call me, sir!' barked the corporal.

'... Bryant, sir.'

'What you looking at me for?'

'I wasn't looking at you, I was looking around at where I was, that's all, sir.'

'Where you are Bryant, is my deck. Who was complaining about the food?'

'I wasn't complaining sir, just that I'm hungry,' said Martin.

'If you want more food you can buy it. If you haven't got money, you can work for it if you get on labour duties. If you ain't on labour duties, you can get someone to leave money at the Angel Tavern at the dockyard, with my name on it. I collect the money for privileges see. Corporal Piggott.'

He looked at us all to make sure we understood the arrangement and then went back to his patrol. Not being able to pay bribes is something else that kills men on prison ships, along with floggings and fever. The further you were away from the captain's quarters the more different the rules were. We sat back down and Martin said, 'Anyone got any money? Right, starvation it is then.'

Bryant kept his eyes on Piggott.

George's body was marked on every side, as if he had been in a war himself. There were sores across it, knots of muscle, and an in-turned foot. I couldn't see how he would ever be up to labour. If he was to lose his chains and get enough to eat he would still need someone looking out for him. The four of us watched the light thin out without saying much at all. The rain had thickened and a wind had marshalled itself to heave up the sea and rock the ship. If we'd had any food down us we would've retched. I thought of the winters ahead, all seven of them. At least the swell roiled the sea such that it moved the muck and eased the stench. An orderly shouted down the deck, 'Look lively, Butcher's coming aboard.'

Some convicts went to the portholes to get a look. I thought it must be someone from the barracks, a marine captain perhaps. What I saw was a ballast-lighter with convicts on it, struggling to get off and on to the gangplank.

A line of four men stomped down to the deck and were greeted by Piggott. He unlocked the gate and let them into our side. The three were covered from their shaven heads to their boots in coal dust. The man in front was vast and stood before us like he himself had been hewed from a mine. He came in close to look at us and the dust on him glinted. He stared at George for a good while and then smiled at me before traipsing off. His name was Butcher and though he was unshackled he must have worn irons for years, for he moved his feet like he was still dragging them, one after the other.

Food was given to each mess to sort out between them. A pint of barley to make soup from, a few pounds of bullocks head or ox cheeks for dinner, a pint of pease between us for supper. I was fortunate with my mess since food was divided fairly. George got less than us, but he wasn't a man. I watched the mess next to us, where even in the murk I could see one man sitting away from his mates, the last to be given and less on his plate. Sunday was string salt pork or beef and it was chapel. God it seems, is always close by punishment. There was daylight in the chapel and it being on the first deck there was better air. The five of us sat at the end of an aisle. I wasn't listening to the chaplain, I was taking in the sunlight that had ventured down the hatches. Then at once it was on my face, warming my cheeks, stroking my shut eyes. But I couldn't find a woodland, a harvest morning, I couldn't find Susanna. I felt a hand shaking my shoulder. Butcher. He shoved past me and let himself down next to George. I must have looked at him curiously but he didn't take a peep at me. I looked to Bryant. I could see he was used to fighting man to man. Free-traders fought with cudgels, muskets and more. They put an end to people who threatened to peach on them. But Bryant didn't seem riled by Butcher. Butcher began whispering to George.

'You want me to see if I can get you out of those irons, do you?'

George nodded.

'Are they feeding you alright, eh? … I'll see you right.'

We sang a hymn, and Butcher ran his finger over the words for George, though he didn't know them himself.

After chapel, there was a flogging on deck. We weren't lined-up to witness it, no charge was read out, no drum was rolled. A man whose bones were already pushing out of his back was shackled to the bars by the turnkey whilst the redcoat Piggott took off his jacket and rolled-up his sleeves. The cat tore his flesh from the second stroke and he cried out through the full dozen. Piggott had enjoyed himself.

'That's what you get for stealing others' food.'

But food was stolen from us by orderlies even before it was handed over, which left some having to steal or beg just to stay alive; and it is better to steal than to beg. The meat was brought to us every couple of days from the slaughterhouse at the dock, the leftovers from every animal. After dinner the turnkey unshackled George. George did not show gratitude nor did he show much relief, for he was not a boy who afforded his feelings much at all. There was some lantern light after twilight which was snuffed-out at nine. The mercy of hammocks is when a ship rolls they don't. We were bunched up like cargo and I'd say I got some sleep about one night in three, being kept awake by lice and the fear of rats the other two. Days were a long drowsiness staggering between sleep and waking. That Sunday the flogged man moaned and yelled through the night the rats drawn to his blood scuttling over him. George always seemed to sleep; it was I think because of his weakness.

I heard his breathing before I saw him. Then there he was, standing over us, leaning over George. Butcher. He clutched George's ankles and dragged him out of his hammock. Then he took him by the arm and began to drag him down his end of the deck. George was unable even to stand on his feet. A moment passed then another and I knew that soon George would ebb into the darkness for good. I hauled myself out of my hammock and swung my chain down on the back of Butcher's head. It sounded like I had brought my shackles down on a log. He only stopped still at first, so I swung a second time. He dropped to his knees, groaning.

'You bastard cur!' he shouted.

There were curses across the deck, as if I had hit a dozen men. A redcoat came through the gate with his cutlass drawn.

In the morning, I was taken to Captain Tench's cabin. I stood before him. He was smartly turned-out, not like the other marines, but often looked low in spirits. His cabin, orderly though it was, still stank like the rest of the hulk.

'We cannot have fighting on a ship Ruse. You know what happens if there's bad blood between men on a ship? The ship cannot run.'

He asked me if I had anything to say. I should have shook my head but he was talking like we were sailing the high seas.

'This isn't the same as a proper ship though is it sir? It's a hulk.'

'Damn it man!' He thumped the table and got to his feet.

'It will be run as a ship whilst I'm its captain.'

I was taken below and given a dozen lashes. Piggott gave them to me. I know he would've hit me harder had he the strength. Butcher stood there and watched, his head bandaged by the surgeon. My messmates too, that I might not cry out, but the last few lashes had me shouting to smother my wailing. When it was over, I had a long look at Piggott's pock-scarred face and I'm happy to say I was looking at it when he took his last breath.

The flogging wasn't all. When meat came to our mess, it was light by up to a pound. The bread short too. I'd once had cause to eat bullock's head in South Petherwin. Susanna had boiled it with ransoms so we could get it down us. It was something to keep you alive, that's all, and not everyone on the hulk could keep it down. Now there wasn't enough of it. Bryant put his hand on the orderly when it was dished out and was threatened with a flogging himself.

'I give you what I'm told to give you,' he said, with a glance in Piggott's direction.

Come night-time Butcher came over again to George, 'You want more food boy, come with me.'

The boy stood up to walk away with Butcher but I held him back. Butcher reasoned, 'Not right that, leaving that boy without enough food when I'm offering to feed him.'

'You take him, you feed him,' said Bryant.

George tugged himself away from me toward Butcher who rested a palm on his head and led him into a corner.

'That ain't right Bryant,' I said.

Martin and Bird said nothing, Bryant just licked his spoon and said, 'There'll be more food for the rest of us then.'

I had to get on my feet, walk away, save me from swinging at Bryant. He looked untroubled by what had just happened. Then he glanced around, front and back, before poking his spoon down an ankle bracelet.

CHAPTER 8

Servant of Servants

'Who here can write?' asked Bryant.

He had a piece of paper the size of a handkerchief, set down on the table, and a piece of charcoal.

'Where did you get this?' I asked.

Me and Martin had been set to untwisting old rope to make oakum for caulking seams in the hull. We had been promised some tobacco in return, and Martin who was longing badly to smoke was pulling with his fingers for all his worth.

'I got it from Piggott,' said Bryant. 'I have to write to get him a little something, so we can be rid of our old wives and maybe do something with the rations.'

'That little something, would it involve grog by any chance?' asked Martin.

'It would,' said Bryant.

Old wives was what convicts called their chains, in their company wherever they went, and Bryant the free-trader, was going to trade some brandy for a divorce.

'I need one of you to write to my brother to make a delivery to Piggott.'

'You think that's what Butcher's doing?' I asked Bryant.

'Butcher's giving Piggott something all right. The only ones from this deck that gets to work elsewhere, and I'd wager it's him that's behind our low rations. God knows what it is he gives him. Now who's going to write this?'

'Can he read, your brother?' asked Martin.

'He knows plenty that can,' said Bryant.

Martin picked up the charcoal and licked the point.

'What's your brother's name?'

'James,' replied Bryant.

'Lovely name.'

Martin began to write most deliberately, Will Bryant dabbed his forefinger on the table.

'Tell him it's you who is writing for me, otherwise he might think it's an excise trap.'

'All right then, what do you want to say?'

'He needs to send a half barrel of brandy to the Angel Tavern in Devonport. Last day of the month.'

'That's it?'

'That's it.'

Martin wrote like he was carving into stone, telling everyone to get out of the light. Bryant prodded the table again.

'Wait. Don't write brandy … write … cream.'

'A barrel of cream?' said Martin.

'Fish then,' said Bryant.

Martin scratched his chin.

'Supposing he sends fish. Piggott won't be happy, will he?' said I.

In the end, Martin put down brandy. The letter had to find its way to north Cornwall, St Ives way, and would take some time. It was handed over to Piggott and we waited in our chains for his brandy to be brought to Devonport. While Butcher and his messmates were working at the dockyard, George was watched by other men on Butcher's behalf. I went near him once and was warned off. George himself didn't look at me. At the beginning of the next month Piggott was smelling of brandy and telling the turnkey to take the chains from us. We got more rations as well and our spirits rose, Bryant's especially. Myself, I was sorrowing because of George. We had let Butcher take him, we had sold him for an extra mouthful of meat that when you threw it at the wall it stuck to it.

With the chains off the three of us were put to work but only on the hulk. We'd do whatever they asked because we wanted to move up a deck to get a chance of working at the dockyard. Whatever Butcher was providing Piggott or the captain, it was more than brandy. Our deck was washed every other day, occasionally Bryant and I cleaned the main deck, making our swabs out of old rope. It was a privilege to be on our knees scrubbing, because we were under skies, even if it rained upon us all day. Bryant and I would try to read the skies for the next day's weather, betting with coin neither of us had. He was a powerful worker and I made a point of drawing the attention of marines towards that fact, for the three of us badly wanted on first deck. One morning we were grafting at dawn as the work party for the dockyard was leaving the ship. Bryant watched all stagger past, down the gangplank and into lifeboats. He would have given a lot to row them to shore, almost anything to be one of them. Last up the hatch were Butcher and his three messmates. Butcher stopped for a moment to look at us and no-one hurried him. He said nothing but he was reminding us of something for sure. Butcher moved on and the captain reminded us of our work, at which Bryant got to his feet and faced Captain Tench, like he were no more than a skipper on a fishing boat.

'We work hard don't we? Always. I want to know why we can't go with the work party. Me and Ruse here could out graft any of them.'

For a moment, Captain Tench looked dumbfounded by Bryant's cheek. Then he took a step forward, right into the bigger man.

'Name?'

'Bryant. Sir.'

'Which deck are you on?'

'We're on the lower deck, which is why I was saying...'

'The work party for the dockyard is from the first deck only.'

As much as I hated him, neither I nor Bryant said a word about Butcher for peaching was beyond the pale.

Sometimes from the top deck we would see rowing boats approaching the hulk, not to come aboard but just to look at it, at us convicts. Nearly all the passengers were women, some standing, passing eye-glasses to each other, some waving, others aghast. Once I got to my feet and waved back and a woman screamed. A redcoat kicked me for it and brandished his cutlass at which Captain Tench chastised him. The captain, young and undersized as he was, was stern and suffered no insolence. He strode-up the deck like an admiral and addressed the boats through a hailer.

'If you have no business with this ship then you should keep away. We will not entertain sightseers. If you persist, you will be arrested.'

They ignored him though, and some boats did have business with the hulk. A young woman was brought aboard, respectably dressed but a working woman dressed for an occasion, with a basket under her arm. She was a bonny young thing but dreary in mood. I didn't look at her long in case I was kicked again, but I saw the captain show her courtesy. I couldn't hear what was said between them as he led her to the bow, but even there the smell was too much for her. An old man was led-up onto the deck, daylight halting his stumbling steps. The redcoat led him to the woman, she took his hand and he looked at her face. The old man looked frail enough to be her grandfather, but could not have been. I surmised he was her father, yet seemed more the child as she comforted him. I began to wonder how I would be in seven years, how much of the South Petherwin farmhand was already lost. She took the cloth from the basket and gave the convict an apple, which he smelt but could not break with his teeth. He grabbed at some bread in the basket and, though the woman appeared to ask questions of him, he could only think of the bread, tearing and devouring it so fast pieces fell from his lips. The woman began to sob and the captain had her led away back to the boat. The basket was taken by a redcoat at which the old man became fraught and was taken below.

Bryant and I were allowed to remain on deck for a while after we had finished scrubbing. The overseer, who had come to take us back down below gave us a smoke of his pipe as we stood looking out to sea. Bryant pointed to a cutter lurching into a headwind.

'He don't know how to tack, look at him. Don't know what to do with the wind. You always have to answer to it, it's the master.'

'You Cornish think you're the only ones who can sail. Well, we have a sea in Devon 'n all,' said the overseer.

Overseer Greenwood was a tall man, so lean he looked fragile. He wore a cloth hat and a black smock to mark him out as one of the half dozen overseers. I had seen him put his knuckle to his forehead as he passed the captain, which made me take him for a seaman himself. Overseers were convicts set apart, with their own sleeping area on the first deck.

Redcoats and even the captain made conversation with them. But they were convicts nonetheless and this man, who constantly half-joked yet looked incurably sad, I took to have been imprisoned for life. He said we had to go below but let us keep the pipe.

Part of the first deck was set aside for the hospital which smelt like a shambles. The folks there had beds of their own, and there was a man to attend to them. Those that could manage the climb were allowed to walk the main deck each day, or just sit in the breeze with their gaol fever. A man retched face down as we walked down the line of beds. When I got to our deck below, George was standing, unguarded, his face against a porthole. There were new clothes on him, hanging off his back and trailing on the floor. I went over to him, Bryant walked the other way.

'George ... George?'

I walked right up to him, tore him away from his daydream.

'You alright boy?'

He turned to face me as a stranger and I saw on his cheek, lit by the porthole, a line of scratches, like a set of ribs.

'What happened to you George?'

Except I knew full well.

'Did Butcher do this, did he?'

He looked to his feet and then shook his head, but I knew he was lying.

'I have to go to my mess,' he said.

I stood in the boy's way.

'You don't need to be in Butcher's mess no more, you can be back with us. We've got plenty of food now, me and Bryant are working. Martin's picking oakum, we got food for yer and no irons.'

I took him over to our table, to Bryant and Martin.

'Be good to have George back with us wouldn't it?'

'It would,' said Martin. 'I could do with those little fingers.'

Bryant was flinty-faced, weighing up George's wounds. The boy's eyes were never still, never upon anything for more than a wing beat.

'Butcher, he won't be able to come near you if you're with us,' I promised him.

'I don't want to be with you James,' added George, in a half whisper.

Bryant piped up, 'No point in forcing the lad.'

George got to his feet and moved silently to Butcher's corner. He walked painfully and obediently, as if Butcher was there at that moment, waiting to drag him into the privy. I grabbed hold of Bryant's smock.

'If anything happens to him!'

'It already has,' he said. 'And I dun't know what we could've done to stop it, except starve.'

His hand reached round my wrist as he pulled it off him.

When it got to evening lanterns were lit. Strangely, winter brought more light to us, as they were lit up and down the deck earlier each day. Butcher you could always hear before you could see him, groaning out his salutations, clumping above us and down the hatch. Piggott opened the gate for him and Bryant got to his feet. The way Will Bryant stood before Butcher, if he had a cap it would've been in his hand.

'Right, Butcher?'

Butcher steadied himself for a stand-off because all encounters for him were like that.

'What do *you* want?'

'I wanna get on your work party,' said Bryant.

Butcher's three messmates, who had gone to their corner heard this and were on their feet like hounds. George too was looking over, to see how this would play.

'Ain't no room,' snarled Butcher.

'Make room then,' said Bryant, nodding in the direction of Butcher's mess.

Butcher just plodded through Bryant dragging one leg after the other. Bryant reached up and put a hand on Butcher's shoulder to turn him half circle.

'Alright, you give me the boy back then. The boy,' said Bryant.

And he took a few strides in the direction of Butcher's mess, before Butcher had him in a headlock, which he broke free by a twist of the arm and began to roll his fists like a boxer might. Butcher, he didn't have a boxer's stance, but I got the impression from his face he'd take any blow Bryant would throw without flinching. Other convicts got to their feet, even the chained, to watch the brawl. There was no Piggott, no redcoat in the passage. Bryant put a couple of jabs into Butcher's face but on the third attempt his fist was clasped in one of Butcher's paws. They were then joined in a wrestling dance, circle after circle.

'Eh, Cornwall! ... Bryant!'

It was Greenwood, the overseer who had given us the pipe from the other side of the bars.

'You haven't seen the hole have you? Haven't been in it. Butcher has, haven't you Butcher? Be going back there 'n all. After a flogging. Piggott's on his way.'

With that, Butcher broke his hold on Bryant and Martin got between the two of them.

'I thought we were going up a deck Will, not the other way.'

If the hole was something Butcher was frightened of it was a bad place. When Piggott came down the hatch he could tell something was awry but no-one said a word. Folks drifted back to their mess tables and Bryant greeted Piggott.

'Evening corporal.'

'Butcher, he's not a sack of spuds is he? More a sack of clay I'd say,' said Martin.

'He's dirt and I'm going to put him in the ground where he belongs,' said Bryant.

'You've enough time in this coffin ahead of you as it is,' I said.

Bryant's face was in his hands. He was, I learned, a schemer and courageous, but also an unruly man, which undid his plans. He brought his hands down to the table and wrung them together.

'I'm sorry about George,' he said. 'I should have done more to keep him with us.'

'Can't blame you for Butcher,' I said, even though I did blame Bryant, but I'd found a weakness and I wanted to use it.

'Listen Will,' I said, 'can you get some more paper, and some ink this time, I wonder. From Piggott? It's for me.'

'You can write can you?'

'I'm Bible read,' I told him. 'And they taught me my letters.'

'Why, who you writing to?'

'Susanna,' I said.

'There's nothing she can do about your situation in here Ruse.'

'It ain't your business what I'm writing to her about.'

I took from his silence that he would at least try and sure enough, I was looking down upon a proper page, ink and quill within a week. Susanna couldn't read so I wrote to the priest, trusting him with my private thoughts. I hadn't seen her since I was for the gallows and I wrote my deepest affections. Susanna had taught me how to give and receive love, she had been a good teacher, more experienced than I, and if that bothered my father it didn't trouble me. I asked about our son, and I told her that there were men on the hulk who had been awaiting transportation for years, that the word was that gaols and hulks were too full and that we might never be sent, but I might well return to her and Richard from Devonport or some other ship, *sooner than you fear my love*. I gave the letter to Bryant to give to Piggott and he told me it had cost him an extra half-barrel of brandy.

The winter took people quickly. They wouldn't wash as much because it meant breaking the ice in the saltwater barrels. Our clothing was no different from the rest of the year and the one blanket they gave us was as thin as a sheet. Convicts did not report men dead in their mess for days so they could enjoy their rations. Gaol fever or the cold took the shackled first for they were lower in spirits. It took those too old to move, to walk the main deck for air. Captain Tench had the decks swabbed each day which only added to men's weakness. He even ordered small bags of gunpowder exploded below to clean the air. Bryant began talking about mutiny and was lucky nobody peached on him. Up on the main deck he had toadied so much that the captain let Bryant inspect the ropes. He would enquire about tonnage and the ship's previous life and at first the captain indulged himself in the fantasy that he was running a real ship, until he saw Bryant's game. One morning when he came on deck, I pointed to the sky and told the captain that I was certain we would get hail. It was a sky I knew well. Cloud high and creamy, bulging like a fleece, beneath it a blue grey haze swirling with a wind.

'Two kinds of men read the sky and you are no seaman, so you must be a farmer.'

'That's right sir.'

'You had a farm at South Petherwin?'

'I did sir,' I went on, not understanding how he knew my village, and my voice sounding strange to me. 'I had a good hundred acres I did, mostly sheep, some dairy, barley where I could.'

He withdrew from his pocket a letter, adding, 'It's from the Reverend Silva at South Petherwin.'

He held it out in front of me but when I reached for it he pulled it away.

'Clearly you won't need me to read it to you,' he said, 'but tell me, how did you get a letter sent from here in the first place?'

'I got someone in the work party to take it out for me,' I said.

'And who provided you with the paper?'

'I gave food to another convict, he obtained it for me.'

He handed me the Priest's reply saying, 'In future Ruse, if you want to write a letter come to me. Your wife will be here in ten days.'

Dear James

It was a fine thing to hear from you and known you are safe. I sleep easily, thinking of you. Your father is keeping Richard and I hear he is well. I am on the parish but getting by, it is not so bad. You must be a good prisoner and a good Christian and then you shall be rewarded. Father Silva will bring me to Devonport and will get a boatman to bring me aboard for to visit you, December 10 or thereabouts.

Ever your wife,

Susanna.

Scant as it was, I felt Susanna's presence in the words, a light from her in the paper I held. So my father had taken in my son but cut my wife adrift. People living off the parish starved during winters. He had never forgiven my marriage, the circumstances of it, Susanna pregnant beforehand. That her family went to neither one church nor the other, that she was older than I, 'well-worn' he called her. I thought there and then of asking the captain for permission to write to my father, to tell him how much I thought of his Christianity, but it would've been to no avail and the captain would have seen it as me chancing my luck.

On the way to my deck I saw George on a hospital bed, the surgeon attending to him with bandages. I could see no more and wasn't allowed near. I asked Greenwood to find out for me and he told me that the boy had broken his arm, that someone had seen him do it to himself, ramming his arm against the bars on a porthole. The hail came pelting in one side, bobbing-off the deck. Two convicts began to pick them up and throw them at each other.

CHAPTER 9

Lust of his Eyes

I looked about the island the following morning. All of it could be walked in a day. I got as high as I could and saw there were hillocks at each end, a sunken centre with marshland and trees. There were two other bays like ours to the south and west; at the edges of our bay, rocky bluffs. I could make out some long-ago field borders but no furrows. If someone had farmed there they'd bred sheep maybe. I watched the mutton-birds come in to nest in their burrows, flying low over the surf breaking on reefs and the shallows of sandbanks. I picked up some dead wood and went back to the camp.

Only McIntyre was there. He had Scottish Jack's neck scarf round his head to keep the sand out of the split in his forehead. I could see Williams out in the boat, tossing his net beyond where the water broke.

'So Ruse, what did you see?' asked McIntyre. 'Any savages out there, sharpening their axes?'

'There's no-one. No-one here but us.'

'That should put Scottish Jack's mind at rest. He's awful nervy about the Maoris.'

'Are you ready to work McIntyre?' I asked.

'I can stand and I can walk, so I can work.'

'I've been thinking,' I said. 'We should divide up. Just for a few days. Me and Williams will go to the rocks over there, you and Scottish Jack, take the next bay. Back here in three days. Things might be easier between you and Williams then.'

'They'll never be easier. Williams isn't right with the world. He's ready to die, has been for a while.'

'That's not surprising is it?

'I didn't know his family were there that night, I swear.'

'He had something worth living for at long last.'

'Well it wasn't me that took it away,' declared McIntyre.

He got to his feet, took a few steps to get his bearing.

'You know Ruse, if Williams were to take a fall on the rocks, you'd be entitled to his take. Let's face it he wouldn't even be here without you. And I've seen how much work you do compared to him. Same with me and Scottish Jack. He spends half his time looking over his shoulder. Thinks he's a big warrior, can't even work. We'd be better off without them. And I'm not saying that because Williams clubbed me.'

His eyes were asking me to join him.

'Are you suggesting we kill them, for their take?' I asked.

He looked pleased by the question.

'I'm saying our take alone won't be enough to buy back the land we lost. Double it and it might. But I say we wait until the month's nearly out before we decide.'

Scottish Jack strode across the dunes with a bag of mutton-birds.

'Easiest meat there is. Put your hands in the burrows, twist their necks.'

We got the fire going and Williams came in with some fish as well. There was more than enough for the day so the un-plucked birds were buried in the sand.

'We're splitting-up,' I said. 'Me and Williams will go east you two west. Back here in three days. You can take the canvas, the water barrel, there's a cave we can use.'

'What about these skins here?' asked McIntyre.

'Just leave them where they are,' I said. 'There's no-one to take them.'

'I thought I heard something last night,' said Scottish Jack.

'When we was sleeping you mean?' asked McIntyre.

'Aye. Somebody walking. Footsteps.'

McIntyre shook his head.

'You were sleeping under the boat, weren't yer?' said McIntyre. 'So, they could've been these two, taking a shit or whatever they get up to whilst we're under the boat.'

Scottish Jack tapped his spoon on his palm.

'It was something or someone that didn't want to be heard.'

'So where are the footprints now?' asked McIntyre.

'Tide's come and gone since,' Williams told him.

'I've just been to look at the island,' I said. 'It's empty.'

Scottish Jack threw down a handful of meat and stood-up.

'If we don't eat something else we'll get the scurvy. I'm going to see if I can get some fern roots.'

'Is it true Jack, that the New Zealand savages are cannibals?' asked McIntyre.

'Watch your mouth McIntyre. Though my brother did tell me once, when they've won a battle the king will eat the eyes of their enemies. It's revenge see. They like to turn their enemies into shit.'

'And you say, they're not savages?' said McIntyre. 'Well, we're their enemies now aren't we, for taking their seals from them?'

Scottish Jack picked up the rifle, 'We are. But they won't touch you McIntyre, because you're already a piece of shit.'

McIntyre shouted after him, 'Gonna shoot those ferns are yer?' He laughed then bellowed out, 'Hel-loooo!'

His shout hung on to the wind.

Me and Williams worked on the rocks for three days, sleeping in a cave. We hadn't carried the water barrel because I had an idea we could drink the water running off the cave walls, but it was brackish. One night I asked Williams, 'Did you mean to hit McIntyre John? I'm not judging you, but I need to know if that's what you're going to do.'

John always took his time in answering. As if, he was working from one language to another.

'I'm glad I hit him. But you have to get enough skins for Evans. So I won't be hitting him again, while we're working.'

Being in charge of men is not something a man can just decide to do. You have to have their permission, or a gun pointed at them.

After three days the foam washed red and we tied what we had to our backs and walked the two miles back to our camp. McIntyre and Scottish Jack were eating the mutton-birds.

'How was the cull?' I asked.

'Fair,' said McIntyre. 'But we've some news for you two.'

'What's that?'

'Well the skins we left here, they're gone.'

'Someone's come and taken them,' added Scottish Jack.

CHAPTER 10

Eye for Eye

An orderly shaved my beard. His hands fluttered and I bled. There was no mirror for me to look at but Martin clutched his pipe and nodded. I had spent every hour of each day thinking about a visit that would last a few minutes; such was the length and the weight of it. The day came with a bright morning and I was allowed to wait up top. The sky was fleshy white and in the mood for snow. I watched the longboats drag themselves towards us, bringing what passed for food and prisoners to be devoured by the hulk. Visits were uncommon; this was a great privilege for me. I saw a boat approaching with a woman on board, the coat I thought I knew, the face I could not make out. Then she took off her hat, the wind combed her hair back and I knew it was her. The oarsmen winched Susanna ever closer towards me. I could see there was no Richard beside her, why was my son not there? I feared the worst of news from her.

Captain Tench greeted Susanna at the top of the gangplank with a slight bow, as if he was welcoming her to an Admiralty ball. She stood nervously, looking every way, covering the front of her face with one hand, carrying a basket in the other. I thought she had become a little smaller in the five months since I'd seen her last. Tench pointed to me, she came over slowly. There was no smile, only the hurt of unhappiness. Though there were convicts and marines about the deck we embraced keenly.

'Richard?' I asked, my face against hers.

'With your father,' she replied. 'He's well he is.'

She pulled away from me, squeezed my arms and hands.

'What of you, James?'

I only nodded.

'I hear such things about these places, terrible things,' she said.

A hatch nearby lifted and two convicts climbed up from below. She stared at the wretches and covered her face again. I felt her waist with my hands and knew her to be famished thin.

'How are things with you Susanna?'

'I'm managing.'

'You're on the parish? You said your mother...'

'Can't feed herself. I have a shilling a week. I won't starve.'

But freeze to death she might.

'I don't have any chains, like some on here.'

I looked down at the basket placed at her feet, she picked it up, I pulled back the cloth, there was food, a pie. I couldn't curb myself and broke into it.

'I'm trying to get a position in a house in Launceston. But there are so many women looking. And younger than me. I'll get something in the end, I'm sure.'

'Eat some of this will you, before I take it all.'

She needed it as much as I and I couldn't get it all down besides, still she shook her head. She took from the basket a book wrapped in cloth, a Bible.

'Father Silva gave it to me for you.'

My hands fumbled over it, Captain Tench nodded in approval. I thought about saying she should sell it on to someone to feed herself, but its loss would have haunted me.

'Thank the father for me, won't you. What about the squire, does he have any work?' I asked.

'You know what he's like. He has his favourites.'

His favourites were women he could tup.

'Father Silva wrote in the letter that my father is keeping Richard.'

'He wouldn't let me bring him here. Probably right, don't you think James?'

'Richard is not his son to decide.'

My fists clenched themselves. Stuck as I was on a prison ship, my father could make me angrier than my captivity.

'Does he let you see him at all?' I asked.

She was dragging her feet on an answer, which was all the answer I needed. I feared losing Richard would sap her will to survive. Without work, without Richard, what would she do? Steal and be transported herself, or worse.

'I might be out of here sooner than we thought,' I said.

'How? How can you get out of here?'

'I'm not talking about escaping. I mean, they have nowhere to transport men to. America is in revolt, Africa is no good, people say they tried it and nobody lasted a month. We can't take any more on this ship and some have been pardoned early to make room. I might be home in a couple of years.'

She didn't believe it and neither did I. I was only months into my seven year sentence. Orderlies and overseers were pardoned, I wasn't even on a work party, was on the bottom deck a sniff away from the bilge and she could smell it on me. While I knew she would give the squire a wide berth, a convict's wife was easy prey to other men, especially masters. Their charity came at a price. A marine called for her to get back in the boat and she was swiftly on her way. I called after her, 'Susanna, you stay alive, you hear me.'

She glanced at me as if I'd slighted her, then I watched the boat heave away with her back to me.

'You alright boy?' asked Bryant.

'You got a wife Will?'

'I like my women too much,' he said.

'That squire I told you about…'

'What about him?' he asked.

'Not only is he fixed on taking all the land, he wants to buy-up the women as well.'

'Like I said James, there has to be a reckoning.'

A vee of geese above us cackled as they neared land.

About injustice Bryant was more ardent than any Methodist I'd met.

'I can feel it James, even on this ship, can't you? Men are thinking of turning on their masters. The unjust have broken a seed from its husk with their greed. It's climbing towards the light when a multitude of shoots will strangle the squires and the generals and the gaolers. Just needs a bit of nurturing that's all.'

Nurture it day and night, he did. He and James Martin, who was sure that Ireland would follow America in revolution, had a particular bitterness concerning religion saying it was *the greatest harness on men's freedom … a tool of the rich to keep the poor in their place.* I defended my faith to him for I know the Gospels and I know Christ, know he was on this earth *a poor man amongst us, leading the poor.*

'Lead you all to your graves, isn't that it?' said Martin. 'You stole didn't you Ruse? Like the rest of us. Where does it say in your Bible you can do that?'

Martin was a carefree blasphemer, Will Bryant more of a persuasive man. He would stand close to me, speak softly.

'You think God wants us to live like this? Look around you, this is an offence to God. Is the king a Christian? His hangmen who stretch the necks of poachers? I say a rising is what God wants from us.'

I laughed out loud.

'You're going to make a revolution on a prison ship two miles out to sea?'

'We can make a stand for ourselves,' he said. 'For better food, clothes, or else we can die here, in another year, two if we're lucky.'

I told him I was going to see how George was and he told me that I shouldn't, for I would be bringing the gaol fever back with me, down to the deck where there was none as yet. Martin, he was of the same mind and voice. A few days later I was relieved of the duty of visiting the boy when Greenwood came to tell me he had passed. We knew of no family to tell, no-one at all.

The hulk had its own graveyard since the rate that people were passing forbad tipping them into the sea. Once or twice a week a small boat with bodies in was towed to the nearest headland and the bodies carried up to a windswept field. I'd asked to be detailed to bury George and rowed myself, Piggott and a private in one boat, dragging the body in a winding sheet in a boat behind. It was a two-mile slog and after a mile the private had to take up one of the oars.

'We don't want to have to bury Ruse 'n all,' said Piggott.

There was a cart at the other end to push up a hill. At the top there was sod to move before I could dig down and when I stopped to rest I looked-up at some woods in the distance, saw myself running, weaving away from shots until the cover of the trees. The private must have read my mind, for he cocked his musket and winked. I got no more than two feet down and Piggott told me to roll the body in. Even little life-less George was too much for me. As I stood over the stooping private, holding a shovel, I thought of driving its point into his neck and then swinging the blade across Piggott's head. I would take a uniform and be away. But schemes are nothing without the readiness to kill a man coldly, like a soldier or an executioner can. I was not that man and I wondered how some were. Will Bryant was such a man, had he been in my place for that moment he would not have returned on the boat. I covered George and spoke the Psalm of David.

Bryant didn't ask me about the burial. I didn't see him leave his hammock late in the night to go to the privy. Nor did I hear Butcher do the same a few moments before. I did not see Bryant return to his hammock, but it could not have been long before we were ordered to rise. There was some alarm down there, the other end of the deck. The orderly was lighting lanterns, felons were on their feet jostling. I swung my legs out whilst Bryant didn't stir, his face though was like a fox's come from the coop; blood on his cheeks and his smock. I heard someone cry 'murder' and I could see Butcher slumped on the privy, bleeding like a stuck pig. The orderly went to fetch the captain. I stood over Bryant as he came past us and spoke softly in his ear.

'Go to the water barrel, wash the blood off your face, turn your smock inside out.'

I went with him, saw one of his arms was red up to the elbow, so dragged the water barrel to the privy and tipped it into Butcher's blood. The captain came and took hold of a lantern. He held it up to Butcher's gaping throat, to men's faces, then he began to walk the deck, peering side-to-side, hammock-to-hammock. He halted, brought the light down on one.

'Which of you lies here?'

A man stepped forward, one of Butcher's messmates called Cantwell, tall and friendless looking. The captain picked-up something from his hammock, held it up before the lantern.

'Is this yours?'

'The convict shook his head.'

'Well it's on your hammock.'

Cantwell's face stiffened with fear.

'Have this man put in irons and brought to my cabin.'

Bryant must have been sharpening the spoon for months, but still he would've had to have driven it hard into Butcher's neck, gripping his head fast for the big man was no sheep. Bryant was silent about the matter and Martin, I believe, was unaware of his guilt. I had no thought for Butcher's life at all, but to do that to Cantwell takes coldness worse than any fury. I had never seen Cantwell talk to anyone, never heard him speak at all. The hulk does that to a man, he sees no purpose in words anymore, his story no more woeful, no more worth telling, than anyone else's. Words bred quarrels and unwanted thoughts. I feared for Cantwell, too sapped to speak-up for himself, I prayed for him. Bryant, he slept easy. Perhaps Piggott knew full well, for he put Bryant and me on Butcher's burial party. I asked that he not be buried beside George and Piggott obliged. A woman came to the graveside, she was tall, very tall for a woman, and Piggott knew her well. For he held her hand to comfort her and I surmised she was Butcher's sister and had been Butcher's bribe to Piggott. I crossed myself, Bryant spat on the ground. As we rowed back, Piggott declared, 'Looks like there's a couple of places on the work party now. But you'll have to play your cards right by me Bryant, understand?'

By this Piggott meant more brandy. For which we got James Martin on the party too, and the three of us were taken with about twenty others to the docks each day to load and unload. There were three wharves with us convicts on wharf one, while others were put in the timber yard next to the slipways, where ships were made and repaired. We had any number of gaffers. Greenwood the overseer, the stevedores we worked amongst, any of whom could give us orders, and the half a dozen redcoats with fixed bayonets who guarded the wharf. The stevedores begrudged our presence and that of the redcoats more. Their gaffer let it be known to the redcoats that his men would only take orders from him, not any man in uniform. The work was heavy and beyond most convicts as we were half-starved. The stevedores would taunt us about how little we could load, how slow we worked. Ships came in from all points west, as constant as the tide, some as large as our hulk. There were so many they would have to wait in the harbour for a place at a wharf. There were spells of rest from time-to-time but men laboured greatly and the strain of the work did kill some, though a day under rain on the dockyard was preferred to any day below decks in the hulk. Seeing crews come in who had passed many horizons, who spoke in other voices with Negroes among them, was close to liberty itself. Once a convict, perhaps overcome with a daydream of freedom, just ran through the redcoats along the wharf and when cautioned to stop he turned only for a moment to look back, then carried on running gaily until musket fire put him down.

The barrels we rolled and lugged were mostly carrying sugar or tobacco, if you couldn't tell by the smell you could tell by the weight. James Martin would put his face close against a tobacco barrel, breathe in hard with his eyes closed, then he'd say, 'As good as a suck on a pipe that,' or, 'It is for the want of a smoke I lost my liberty.'

One time a three-mast vessel came in so overloaded with barrels from the Caribbean we could smell her a quarter mile away. There were merci-less looking men among the crew, faces baked to crusts, clothes no less ragged as ours. The head stevedore and half-a-dozen others boarded her carrying their tackle and hooks, they went below, and soon they came up and raised a commotion, running to the gangplank shouting, 'Hold fast, she's a slaver! A slaver.'

We were warned not to touch her, not to lift a barrel. The captain called the harbour master who told the stevedores that if they didn't unload her they wouldn't be unloading anything else, for ships would just head for Bristol instead. Still they stood down. The harbour master even shouted at Greenwood our overseer to *get your curs to work*, but

Greenwood knew if he gave any such order it would have been tinder to a riot. Then Bryant spoke up, so everyone could hear, 'We convicts are little more than slaves ourselves, why would we toil for those that enslave others? We shall stand alongside the stevedores, won't we?'

His words changed nothing, for we were never about to unload the ship on our own, but Will Bryant had staged himself as the rebel, which was his purpose. The matter was settled as the stevedores agreed to unload as long as it was to be the last slave ship to use the wharves. On the hulk that evening Bryant was lively with plans of rebellion.

'We should do what the stevedores do. Stop work, stand fast until our demands are met.'

'We are all so scrawny they'd work better without us,' I said.

'What are our demands exactly?' asked Martin.

Bryant pushed out a finger with each demand.

'We need better garments, better food, blankets…'

Martin interrupted him.

'We need those with gaol fever to be treated somewhere else. Not on this ship. Tis spreading fast so it is.'

Bryant nodded, he had at least one accomplice.

Winter crept on towards Christmas and word came that Cantwell had been hanged for Butcher's murder. His other two messmates took the news severely. One of them said to me, 'Who would bring a blade back to their own hammock? I went and said such a thing to the captain but he said it was with the judge now. But a judge never looks no further than the dock. The man who killed Butcher is still on our deck.'

There was no way of telling or asking what he knew.

The work on the wharf made some of us stronger, others weaker. Even after we'd finished, I felt like I was pulling a plough through a sodden field. When I tried to swing out of my hammock, I was wearing a suit of armour. What the work did though was gobble up the days. A month would go by in what felt like a week before. Some ships, especially the schooners would be back in half the time of other ships and their crews, gratified to be on land again, would greet us, smile and say, 'Don't you be in a hurry to load her up again.'

The stevedores were clannish. To most, we were invisible, to some we were to be despised as thieves, to a few we were to be pitied. When some of our men were in bare feet, even when the ground was coated in ice, their gaffer handed over clogs the next day. Greenwood our overseer was against conversation between the two groups, and if it was more than a few words we were likely to feel a musket butt in our ribs. Some stevedores asked after convicts on the hulk, at first I thought they must know them until Bryant twigged they were passing messages to loved ones. I saw Bryant myself exchanging words three times with the same man who gave Bryant some grub for his pocket. I said to him, 'You know that man Will?'

'That James, is a true Christian,' he replied.

Christmas could not be kept by us other than by recalling the Christmases past. James Martin spoke of the farm he was raised on in Antrim, where food was ample. How his favourite dish was hare, cooked by his mother with apples and onions and cream. Then he talked us through other meals: baked fowls, honey cakes, bacon chine, some praying, plenty of singing. The light-headedness of my hunger nigh on made me pass-out. Bryant's family spent the holy day drinking from morning to night. And fighting sometimes too. December is a lean month for a farm labourer, there was no feasting for me and Susanna. But I have memories of being a small boy, my head just above the table edge, on my father's farm in Lawhitton, before my mother died. There was a fire burning, a good fire. She walked towards it, not walking well and steadying herself on the hearth as she tended it. She began a song, her back to us. *There was an old woman tossed-up in a basket, seventeen times as high as the moon.* My brothers joined in, I had food in my hand. Come evening our father would tell us a story from the Old Testament.

Christmas Day we were all in the chapel for a good part of it. The minister said that Christ was born this day to grant us everlasting life and then announced that two more convicts had died this morning. We prayed for their souls.

'Pray for more food and clothes more like,' whispered Martin.

When we went to our deck, Will Bryant spelt out his terms.

'Right, that's it,' he said. 'Tomorrow, first vessel in, we board it. We don't get off it til they promise better rations and some blankets.'

'And all men with something on their feet, the sick off this ship,' added Martin.

'Won't the redcoats have something to say about all this?' I said.

'They'll have weak heads from the night before. The ship will be ours before they can raise a hand, after that play it by ear,' said Bryant. 'We make a stand, say our piece, that's all. When they cock their muskets, we disembark.'

'The stevedores might stand with us,' said Martin.

I nodded. 'They just might.'

I was for it. It felt just, more so than stealing from a coiner. Butcher's killing wasn't enough. There were other boys, orphans and urchins, taken out of sight to be buried on board, then to the field ashore. I had more than another three years on the hulk and I doubted I would see those years on what they were giving me. I'd kept animals better than the prison ship kept me.

When we were taken to the wharf the day after Christmas, the stevedores were already unloading a vessel, its cargo rolling towards the warehouse. But this gave us time to pass the word to other convicts for most of the work party was from the deck above and were not in the knowledge of the plan.

'We board the next ship for bread and blankets,' was muttered from ear-to-ear.

Waiting in the harbour was a two-mast brig carrying with the scent of coffee. It was the stevedores who tied her up and waited by the edge of the wharf for the crew to land. I looked over my shoulder at Bryant, who gave me a nod as if to say *whenever you like*. Then as the first stevedore put his foot on the gangplank, Bryant roared out, 'Board her!'

We convicts charged our way through the stevedores and onto the ship. Martin was first on board and when we were all there he tipped the gangplank away and the cry went up, 'Bread and blankets! Boots and smocks! Convicts are not slaves!'

It was a stirring sound, a joyous spectacle to behold. We felt blissful as if all at once filled with the Holy Spirit. The stevedores stood stranded on the wharf, some cheered us. I looked about for Will that we might smile to one another but couldn't see him. I wondered if we were half-way up a mast but he was nowhere on the ship or the wharf. Martin shouted out our demands, about food, clothing, and the sick. He said we were keeping the ship and would help ourselves to the cargo until we got the answer we wanted. It wasn't long before the marines came forward, three of them kneeled, the other three stood upright. They cocked their muskets.

CHAPTER 11

Farewell

Martin had one ear to the floor, a hand over the other, his face frigid as a painting.

'What can you hear?' I asked.

He held out his arm to shut me up. Then he scuttered a yard or two, put his head down again. All of a sudden he jolted-up like he'd been poked in the face. He knocked on the floor with his knuckle.

'He's here, just here. Must be.'

He stood and stamped his feet. I thought he was about to dance.

'Get me some water will you?'

I steadied the ladle down the deck to him, he trickled the water between the boards at his feet. I didn't drink the water for I believed it carried the fever, but below where we stood Bryant wasn't about to get any small beer. Martin dipped down again, lay this time, trying to see through the cracks in the boards, he kept knocking then looked-up at me smiling.

'Did you hear that? He's there.'

I hadn't heard a whisper. I wondered if Martin really had.

'Will, Will, are yer there?' he called.

Will Bryant had been put below the lowest deck, in the ship's hold, in a box not big enough to bear the name cell, below the water line. It was January and he'd been there a week. He'd been nabbed on the road beyond Plymouth, the same day he ran, wearing a stevedore's coat. He'd never boarded the brig with us, never took part in his own revolution, just his one-man escape. I wondered if that was his plan all along, if all the talk about turning the world upside down was just a way to have everyone looking the other way while he slipped the net. If it was, he was a clever fish.

I'd not known the hole used before then. Convicts had spoken of it dreadfully but the captain hadn't had cause. Anyone who tried to escape was bound to be punished hard, a flogging they might not survive, for Bryant it was a spell in a sitting coffin with only the ballast beneath him. We thought he would die and Martin and I knocked on the deck floor, called out to him morning, noon and night. We poked pieces of food between the boards. I would hear Bryant tap back and I would hear his voice but I couldn't understand him. I think the box they had him in was well to the stern, beyond the bulkhead at the end of the deck. James Martin was lucky he didn't get the flogging. He had led the charge and he had issued the demands but, when the muskets were cocked, he led us all off the ship. Captain Tench knew what we had done, and why, though it was a long time before we heard anything about our demands.

From after that Christmas we were never allowed ashore as one work party again. We were split into three groups, one for each wharf, with me and a handful of men sent to the boatyard. All of us had a yellow square sewn on our smocks. I was to help build the captain a boat. The ship's carpenter gave the orders with me in the sawpit. It was to be a sloop, for the captain's pleasure alone. He came to inspect progress and said to me, 'You miss the land don't you Ruse? Farming, making something grow out of the earth?'

'I do sir.'

'Well I miss sailing, the sea. Out there where we are is not the sea. It's a stew. Sailing is a way of harvesting the sea.'

Up to then the only wood I'd worked with was willow and hazel, but I learned all about grain and about steaming larch wood to make it bend. We took our time with it all and I never thought of escape, not with the slow death of Bryant below us. Then one afternoon I came back on board and there was what I thought was a great dog lying on the deck, its legs curled up, shivering from shoulder to feet, covered in filth, by a stove. It was a man, it was Will Bryant. He was shaking and his eyes were closed against the scant light on deck for there had been none where he'd been for the last month. Many of us, especially those that toiled on the docks, looked as grubby as beggars tramping through my village, but Bryant he looked more like a beast. Piggott was sat on his stool chewing tobacco, looking on from behind his blank, craggy face. I shouted to the orderly to heat some water and some broth, who looked to Piggott who nodded. I washed Will, I scrubbed him with a brush, I had to ask for more water and fetch him a new smock and trousers. He couldn't stand on his own, his legs buckled like a newborn lamb. I sat him on his hammock with his legs dangling over the side like a hung turkey's, I rubbed them for him.

'Try not to lie on your back, with your legs up. Get some blood into them.'

I could make out Bryant's ribs, he was scrag and hatchet-faced, but there was always a flame burning away inside him that couldn't be put out, no more than you could stop a wild rose coming into bud. The stove arrived the same day as him; I told him it was because of him, it was his victory.

It took us to the summer to make the captain's sloop and he came to the slipway himself to launch her. The captain, the carpenter and myself took her out into the middle of the estuary, into the sound, where the water was swirling. It was a small thing with one mast, a main and a headsail. Snug as it was it could turn quick in the water and the captain was like a small boy, playing his rudder in the wind. I'd fished from a boat on the Tamar with my father and swam in the river too, but that was where it wasn't much wider than the deck. Here we were so far from the shore we might as well have been out in the sea, the captain only enjoying it when a wave lapped over the sides.

We were given a little payment for our work, with which we were allowed to buy small beer and tobacco, the tobacco I gave to Martin. What I wanted more though was the favour of sending another letter to Susanna and, much more, another visit. I was permitted the letter.

Father Silva

I hope I find you in health. I remain strong. I write to ask of news of my Susanna and my son Richard. Her visit here last year was of great comfort and relief to me though from when she left me I have since been worried about her health and spirits. Also my son Richard is with my father and has not seen his mother which will be of great distress since he loves his mother dearly. All sons must be with their mothers. Thank you for the Bible it is of comfort to me. I know God is always with us.

James Ruse.

Captain Tench read it through before he sealed it, his face remaining firm, his thoughts distant.

'I will send it for you.'

Bryant, though we would have had to carry him, would not go to the hospital deck. He shook all the nights next to me for days. I made him stand each morning and I helped him walk further each day. He trod like Lazarus, each little step a marvel. When we came back from the wharves he was always sitting on a stool staring into the stove, never looking away. He became silent, knowing he would never be allowed off the hulk to work again. He was left with years to kill and nothing to kill them with. I treated the passing of time like cutting a large field, one you couldn't see the end to. It's all there before you, you just have to start, get into a rhythm with your scythe. After a short while the shoulder will begin to get sore and you think of stopping but you mustn't. Pain becomes part of the rhythm you work with, always look down and never up or back. Go slow and leave it as long as you can until you figure how far in you are. The pain I carried was waiting for a reply to my letter to Father Silva.

When it came to winter again, we were given another blanket and something warmer to wear. A man came in a top hat and tails, was shown round the ship by the captain and asked questions of orderlies, Greenwood and convicts. The answers he wrote down in a book. By Christmas, the very sick were taken off the ship, there were carrots and beans in the broth, and the chaplain was ordered to teach the boys their letters and numbers every afternoon. I asked him if I could take part but he refused me. For the chaplain, there was no redemption in this life. The Bible for him was about the past, Christ was not alive, we were in a queue for death. He was a man as much in need of comfort as us.

Maybe around half a year after my letter to Father Silva, he wrote back. The letter, whatever its news, I knew would weigh heavy on me for some time, but I had not foreseen what was written there.

James Ruse,

I write at last to tell you your son is well though not with his mother. Susanna still lives where you once lived with her. She is paid for by the parish the sum of six shillings a month now, for she is mother to another child, a daughter Elizabeth born this September. The father is recorded as Doctor Strong jnr though the family does not acknowledge Elizabeth by way of any money or kind. Susanna did not want me to write to you but I felt I must act against her wishes. I have waited until the child was born to see if she thrived, which she does. Although this news must be a great burden to you, you must search in your heart for forgiveness. Remember the words of Psalm Twelve.

I remain your Priest,

Father Silva.

I had no forgiveness to look for. A convict's wife is prey to men, for she is likely poor, near destitute maybe. But Susanna was not feeding and clothing our son, and she was young enough and able enough to work. I'd seen the young doctor trotting about, dainty on a chestnut horse. Could she have been sick, I wondered. Except he and his father would sooner tend to a squire's sick calf than a poor woman. What was she thinking? That he was interested in keeping her, wedding her? That he would take her about in respectable company? Susanna was not wet behind the ears, he was younger than me, if it was force she could have fought him, he was skin and bone, a scarecrow in velvet. And to have given this base-born bastard the name of our first-born child who had not lived but three weeks. And my mother's name too. Susanna had lowered herself for certain.

The letter went into the stove. Bryant's eyes bid me a question but I said nothing, never spoke of it, to him or Martin, the chaplain or the captain. Where would I go in five years' time? Back to my father perhaps, if he was still alive; and to my son Richard, who would not know me. I could not imagine returning to South Petherwin, facing Susanna, the village, of ever having a farm there, or even a place in my own country. Bryant's words about masters and tyranny seemed plain and true. England was an unjust land for working men; we were not free to live off common land anymore, even to glean after harvest, not allowed a place in the shire in return for our labour. Land was taken from us, rights to hunt game too, hope it seemed also; even my own wife. The prison ship, the men inside it, that was the only society I could know.

In the spring of the following year, news came of a convict ship to America that had been taken off Spithead. They'd tried to sail her to Ireland but storms drove them back to England. A few got away, some were hanged, the rest sent to hulks, a dozen to ours. The war with America was at an end it was said, and I did not dread being taken there. The mutineers were cheered on board, men stamped their feet in praise of them when they were brought on deck. They told their tale each day, were listened to, lauded, swaggering the deck like pirates in chains. They were fearless, abandoned men who had struck out, chancing their lives, almost prevailing. The worst wolves among them were from London; Godless people, thievery in their veins. We didn't like them, Bryant, Martin and me, for they switched the pecking order with us Cornish no longer at the top. One among them was a boy, Barrett, his face blank like an owl, his features severe, his manner flinty, yet he had great craft, greater than any convict I've known. He would carve things out of wood, could engrave into spoons, images of us, inscribe them too, and he did this all with irons on his arms. They were exchanged for food, beer anything he fancied.

'Got a sweetheart?' he asked me. 'You tell me what she looks like and I'll carve her likeness. What's her name then?'

'There's no sweetheart. There was a wife. But not now.'

'She's gone has she? Shame. Still I'll make you a token you can remember her by.'

'Where did you learn to do that?' I asked him.

'I drew a lot of pictures of the king see. Like my ol' dad, who they hanged for it. You want a token or not?'

He was a coiner, and a better one than Thomas Olive. Maybe they had a keener eye in London, maybe they minded less where money came from in Cornwall.

Sometime after, another group of convicts was sent to us who created great turbulence and unquiet; a small number of women. They were more unruly and rowdy than men, they never ceased cat-fighting, they had pitchforks for tongues. They were behind bars at the stern but would howl down the deck, taunt and curse. Piggott and his men were supposed to keep order, keep us away from the bars but they preferred the entertainment. Piggott would bait the women until they cursed him as a *bastard of a dog,* or *a shamble-legged molly that lies with men,* at which he would throw a tub of water over them. But they lifted Will Bryant's spirits for he loved their boldness and he loved the sight of them, mucky though they were. Bryant never left the deck and as soon as he was able to walk again they put irons on his legs for six months. He would hold himself up at their bars and gab all day, his tongue as quick as any of theirs. Many of the women were Cornish, some from further west than he and possessed of more fight. He struck up a fellowship with one who was from Fowey, Mary Broad her name, still girlish but with child. She had red curls rolling off her shoulders, winter blue eyes, a face a little marked by pox, and a knee that faced in. Bryant put it around the deck that she was to be looked-out for, given what food could be spared. Come the night he would tell me what they had spoken about, how her family were free-traders, her brothers, ruffians. There was laughter in his voice, which I'd never heard in three years. He even got Barrett to make her a love token; a flower cut into the back of a spoon. He never asked about the father of the child.

One morning, about a month after the women had come, Piggott came down with a list. He called out names; mine, Bryant's, Martin's, Barrett's, twenty of us all told, including women, but none above a certain age, none that couldn't work. Piggott told us, 'You're all going on a little voyage, to London, to a hulk there. Tomorrow, be ready, say your farewells today.'

I knew this to be the beginning of a longer journey. They had already tried to send Barrett and others there; they had put the women with us. We all expected to be sent to London to be put aboard a ship for Georgia, there to work with the slaves. Bryant, his only worry was whether he would be with Mary Broad from Fowey. I said goodbye to Greenwood, the overseer. For all his years imprisoned, he had not let it harden him. And also to Captain Tench, for not many prisoners were allowed the privilege of letters and, having read mine, he knew my extra sorrow. For once, he smiled.

CHAPTER 12

Exodus

May 1787

I saw my mother lying in the berth across from mine, her legs and arms in irons, bloody sores at the bracelets. She writhed about, assailing the boards; she screamed my father's name.

'Richard, Oh Richard, help me! Husband, where are you?'

A man walked up the aisle between us, his white sleeves rolled, blood to his elbows. I called out to her, 'Mother it is James. James. I am here.'

I could not reach out my arms for they were too heavy.

'James,' she cried, 'James is that you?'

'Yes mother, it is I.'

A voice from someone lying next to me asked, 'Why did we ever leave them?'

I awoke and turned to him, he said, 'Will we feel the same about Mother England I wonder? Torn from her womb and cast to the edge of the earth.'

He was a well-spoken man, his voice softened by education and comfort. Even in his convict clothes, he had a gentleman's appearance. His name was Charles Peat, Mr Peat as he liked to say and he lay to the right of me as far as Cape Town. He was a highwayman but also a *Mercury* man, one among the mutineers confined on our ship. Those first few days of the voyage, whilst we were in irons, I never left my berth, except to do the necessary, and Mr Peat's voice, close by and polite, consoled me, no matter what the words.

'They have dreams of their own James, the men who are taking us away. They believe they can make a great civilisation in a land of savages, as great as the civilisation once was that we have left behind. That world is now dying, drowning in blood and in tyranny like Rome did so they must plant anew. I know this because I have met these men, dined with them, spoken to them in their coffee houses in London. They have visions that are beyond them. They believe they can rule the earth and even the oceans in-between, but they are mistaken, don't you think?'

There was much wailing and cursing those first days, men called for their mothers caring not who heard them, but Peat remained composed which was a comfort to me. Neither did he retch at all and was tolerant of my retching.

To my left lay a man caged by fear. He was scrawny, scarred, still as the dead, his eyes held open, prepared for some cruelty. There was burning around his ear and he had been branded on his cheek. Just to glance at him was to condemn him, and I heard him mutter from time-to-time.

'I didn't take it, who saw me? Someone said they saw me, don't believe them boss.'

He would lie with his knees up, hands over his face.

After a few days, we were freed from our irons and in groups of ten taken up to the main deck to walk around. I had never been upon the sea before, in its midst. I had looked at it from the cliffs at Tintagel once with my father. Out in the distance a fishing boat was being hurled about, he said to me, 'Men that work the sea are brutes James. They haven't the patience or the knowledge to work the land. They are lonely men who hold their lives cheaply. A man's living is to be made from land.'

I stood on the deck and looked in dread, in reverence at the marvel of the sea and of the men that worked upon it. We convicts fought to keep upon our feet whilst they skipped the rigging and worked sails in a wind that dragged a ship full of three hundred men. They were squirrels moving along the high masts, calling out all the while. Some convicts clung to the mainmast retching where they stood, a seaman, a black, threw water at their feet, and pointed to the side of the ship, but they only gripped the mast tighter. We stared out at the mounting waves, the horizon dipping then rising, dipping then rising. Our eyes watered with the wind, wondering how long before our vessel was broken into firewood. In the distance, either side of us, were several ships of the fleet and on the deck of the nearest stood convicts who were women. Across the reach of water, I could hear lewd cat-calls back and forth. Behind us lay a line of moss.

'Let's not look away until she's gone James. England. Gone from our eyes but not our hearts.'

Peat had brought his blanket to the deck and was one of the few able to steady himself with the roll beneath him.

'That ain't England,' I said to him, 'that's Cornwall.'

'Indeed.'

He looked up to the quarterdeck above us where a line of marines were stood with fixed bayonets, and Peat was cogitating, scheming.

It was New Holland to which we were being taken, not America. I had been told this in Portsmouth. It is a land that was not drawn on the Sunday school globe, a land the extent of which is not known. Mr Peat took his plate and held it up as the face of the earth, marking out the edge of lands in the grease.

'This here James is England, and here the rest of Christendom. Over here are the Americas, little more than a wilderness of Indians, cannibals and rebels. Here, Africa, India and the East. And hereabouts,' his palm held out below the plate, 'is where we are being taken.' He tossed the plate to the floor. The redcoat on the hatch ladder shouted, 'You. Pick up that plate or you'll be flogged.'

Peat obeyed and addressed the redcoat.

'It will be a miracle if we survive the journey, if we last six months in the Garden of Eden. Any of us.'

The marine spat.

'That's mutiny talk that is. That could be a hundred lashes.'

'Sir, I have no intention of inducing a revolution. I'm only stating what you know to be true.'

Peat stooped away, and the redcoat spat once more.

'You're a Mercury man, don't think I don't know that,' he shouted.

There was a redcoat below to watch us at all times, except for the minutes when one replaced the other, at which times some men would curse and strike others. We were crammed into the lowest deck, below the marines and crew, with the stench of ballast and bilge, of ourselves, stuck to our throats. The redcoats on guard would tie a scarf about their faces to ward off the foulness. When the bell rang for a change of guard, the fearful man to my left went to Peat, spoke as in the manner of a confession.

'I was in Virginia, seven years I was a slave, branded see, for I ran, I ran twice, and that was a branding.'

He placed a finger against his cheek where a letter R had been burned in.

'The Indians there, they ate what we ate.'

'What did your owners have you do?' asked Charles Peat.

'Cut down trees mostly, make their farms for them. The Shawnee fired arrows at us for it.'

He took off his shirt and showed us where the arrow had entered, but all I could look at were the welts from past floggings, the brand on his face. He was a ravaged soul. Other convicts circled to look-on and listen.

'They hunted in the woods and the settlers, they cut them down. Some slaves ran away to live with the Indians, but they killed them.'

'What is your name?' asked Peat.

'My name is John Williams.'

Williams' eyes beseeched Peat like a pleading dog.

'John Williams, your suffering has not been for nothing. It serves as a lesson to the rest of us.'

'I'm hoping the people will be kinder to us in Botany Bay.'

Peat placed his hand on Williams' furrowed shoulder.

'My boy, there *are* no people there. They say we will be the first.'

Williams grinned, 'Then we can all be good to each other.'

A moment later Peat said to me, 'He's touched that boy, but he may bring us luck.'

Each day on deck, I looked at the colour and the temper of the ocean, judging it against the day before. I looked at it the way I used to look at leaves come September. I knew it was all fashioned by the light which was shepherded by clouds and those in turn by the wind. Wind is soil to a sailor, granting and denying life. When measured against the weeks, the breeze became warmer; the sun more fierce as we headed south, a scent came to the air, of southern lands and the bounty that grew there.

I saw fish that left the sea for the air, great numbers of them flying from the water. Dolphins leapt in pairs about the ship, were harpooned by the crew, hurled on board to gasp and waggle out their time. Jacob the black stuck a shark, it taking three men to rope it in. They winched it up from over a yardarm and swung it over, its blood dripping onto our heads. It was a ferocious sight but pleasing to the crew for shark meat was better than the rations. Whenever the chance arose Williams would exchange words with Jacob. I saw him point out his brand. Perhaps Williams thought Jacob a slave, believing they had lived a life in common. He took off his shirt to show Jacob the scars and Jacob turned him around and called over other seamen, who asked him questions until ordered back to work. Jacob himself was no slave, masters and mates spoke kindly to him, and he wore about his belt a hatchet and a blubber knife.

The captain spent much time peering through his telescope at the other ships in our fleet and into far-flung weather. You could see him conversing with his lieutenant about cloud and wind and water, pointing to the flight of birds. Any storm, even one seen in a telescope, sends forth its heralds in gusts and showers, phantom waves that can catch a crew unawares. And so it was with a flint-coloured sky behind us one morning, a wave tipped us like a bucket and sent a convict sliding overboard into the abyss. A shout went up, a seaman ran to the side with a rope, but there was no-one to throw it to. Then a flying fish landed on the spar deck. It sprung about until someone knocked it dead. We went back below and the storm threw us out of our berths for two nights. There was cursing and praying, but the lost man was no more talked about, or any more pitied than the flying fish.

It was the month of June when we saw the island of Tenerife. The heat below was murderous for the hatch was always sealed on us and only when we or others were let up top was there anything fresh to breathe. We would crowd about the steps without our shirts for a moment of relief. Our water ration of three pints a day left us gasping, and the heat took two men. On deck, we tied our shirts about our heads against the sun, looking towards the mountain that rose over the island; a magnificence I had not seen before.

'How can it have snow on its top in this heat?' I asked Peat.

'Maybe the heavens are not as warm as we think,' he said.

Arrival at the island brought solace to the crew, some comfort to the convicts. It was land, and some questioned whether the fleet knew its path at all. Small boats rowed out in the harbour to greet us, throwing on fruit, asking to come aboard. We were sent below and heard the anchor plunge, at night we heard the crew sing to a fiddle. Peat leaned across me to speak to John Williams.

'John, John. Your friend, the negro seaman, what is his name?'

'Jacob. His name is Jacob.'

'And what is he like?'

'Jacob's from Madagascar. It's an island, with pirates and slaves and great sailors. He has been to America.'

Williams was boasting like a child and Peat's eyes rolled.

'Interesting, but that's not what I meant. Do you think he would allow you to borrow that hatchet he wears about his belt? I only ask because, you see, if we had hold of it we could open the hatch at night to get some air.'

Williams didn't answer, he was too fearful to say one thing or another. The next day two other *Mercury* men, Farrell and Griffiths, struck him fiercely saying he had better do it soon or else he'd be wearing more scars.

On deck, we were close enough to the harbour to hear church bells ring, women laugh, to smell charcoal fires. The captain knew every convict imagined joining them in their freedom, and our time up top was cut in half, always we were guarded, troublesome convicts put in irons. He ordered us to eat figs, something I hadn't seen before or since, told it would see off the flux.

I didn't hear anything said between them, but two days into our stay at the island, Mr Peat was much in counsel with Farrell and Griffiths and John Williams was never still with agitation, never quiet through the night. Come one morning he was restless to get on deck and when he got there he caused a stir, walking around in circles muttering, taking figs from the barrel, throwing them at Jacob. It all turned an officer's head. I placed my hand on John Williams' shoulder, he said to me, 'Three hundred lashes on my back. Three times they whipped me, after the second time they had to wait until I had a back to whip. All for the word, just that word alone,' he whispered it into my ear, '*mutiny*.'

He took another fig and threw it at Jacob shouting, 'He's not a slave no more, so he won't be whipped.'

'Seize that man!' ordered the officer.

John Williams was put in irons and flogged two dozen strokes by the bosun's mate. His flesh was torn at the sixth stroke and he fell to his knees after the first dozen crying out, 'Please God, send me mercy.'

They were flogging his soul and it had been hanging on a cross for years. A search was made below and the hatchet found. Farrell and Griffiths were put on another ship to be flogged, Jacob and some other crewmates deserted for the island. Whether it was true or not, all below believed John Williams had peached on Jacob and the *Mercury* men.

The sea had more humours to show us. There were many days of the calms, when the ocean would not heave and wind came in cupfuls. The sluggishness brought on spells of silence above and below. The crew didn't shout and the convicts didn't gabble; everyone was waiting. One morning without a sniff of wind or a shrug of the ship, a sailor fell from a yardarm; you could hear his bones break on the deck. We saw lightning slash the skies but no rain came to us. And though we had just taken some on, water rations were cut.

Charles Peat didn't say a word for weeks after Jacob's hatchet was found, then as though in reply to a question, he said to me, 'You know that Farrell and Griffiths were seamen? Some of the crew would have been with us. If we had taken the ship we'd be almost at America by now.'

'Redcoats would have slaughtered the half of us,' I said.

'How long have you been transported for James?'

'Seven years, but I already served four on a hulk.'

Peat nodded as if he was looking at the map of my life.

'Then if you survive a year down there, it'll be time for you to go home. Do you think they'll let you?'

'They'll have to,' I said. 'That's my sentence.'

Peat smiled, I amused him.

'You think the captain has the records in his cabin, do you? All our names written down, with a number next to them? James, we are being sent to Botany Bay not as a punishment but as a means to possess the land. That was why convicts were sent to America. They want us to make the wilderness into a farm, to tame the natives and breed amongst ourselves. We are livestock James.'

I didn't like what he was saying, but it wasn't just more of Bryant's rebel talk either.

'I will see Cornwall again, I know I will.'

Some below was too tired to take their walk up deck, they lay all day and night in their berths and I could see that after three months out the disease of the hulk had come aboard, the scurvy. Williams was bleeding from his mouth and I fed him the flesh of figs for he was always only half-awake, possessed by his own ghost. When we made harbour at Rio, oranges were brought on board, thrown down below at us. Peat peeled one for Williams telling him, 'You must survive this journey John, for at its end lies your redemption.'

Whatever Peat believed Williams had said to officers he had forgiven him, for he took such pity on his fear and suffering. As we sailed east the nights were ever cold and a convict took Williams' blanket without a word of complaint saying he would, 'Strangle the traitor the minute we land.'

'Why don't you just do it now,' asked Peat, 'while the redcoat isn't here? This is your chance, no-one will tell.'

The convict had a picture in his mind, Peat interrupted his thoughts.

'It is because you can't do it in front of us, so shameful it would be.'

Whales followed us east and a great many fish were caught, enough that we were given their meat. Many convicts, hungry though they were, refused it, fish an unknown food to them. I ate pieces of albacore, its meat like game. One day a strange blue creature was netted, with horns above its eyes and a mouth like a tankard. It was speared and cut apart, and whole fish were found inside it, still perfectly alive.

At the Cape of Africa, *everything that creepeth upon the earth* was taken on board the fleet. From below, we could hear the sounds of sheep, pigs, chickens, and hooves. It was as if we were leaving for a world barren of plants and animals. On deck, I watched a tormented horse tugging at the end of a rope. The marine's remedy was to lay on with the whip. From the quarterdeck above us, a wig wearing officer shouted down, 'Yardsley, Ruse, show yourselves!'

We walked forward, tugged our forelocks. He ordered a redcoat, 'Take these two.'

We were put in a boat and rowed away. I believed we were suspected of some conspiracy and had been seized for a flogging. Alongside the hull of another ship I could hear the screams of childbirth. We were put upon the *Supply* and taken to the stern. There we stood before an officer, who looked to me like the ship's captain, who I later found out was the commodore of the whole fleet. Next to him, stood a shorter barrel-chested man in a white shirt and black waistcoat. Only he spoke to us, thumbs poked into his pockets.

'Which one is Ruse?'

'Me sir.'

'You had a farm in Cornwall?'

'That is right sir.'

'Your task is simple. Keep our livestock alive that they may keep us alive when we get there.'

Two hens fussed about his feet. A goat looked-up from the quarterdeck. All the way to the forecastle, jostling about the crew, were pigs, cattle, a pony, turkeys, geese, goats. He picked up a hen and tossed it down to the quarterdeck, then he scuttled about for the other but could not catch it for he was an older man. Yardsley picked up the hen and stroked it. The man straightened himself, tucked his thumbs back into his pockets.

'The carpenter is making pens, but animals need exercise as men do. On the lower deck there is hay and feed and a collection of plants and seeds. Yardsley, you will tend the plants as if they were your babes in arms. You will be the only convicts on the ship, here for the cargo, you report to me. You will sleep in the crew's quarters and I advise you a Jack is apt to slit the nose of a thief. My name is Mr Henry Dodd, you will call me sir.'

'Sir, may I ask sir,' I said, 'how long is it to New Holland?'

'Two months give or take.'

Once we sailed the animals became ever more troubled, like I'd always imagined them to be on Noah's Ark. Troubled creatures, like troubled men, die before their time. I would have to give them as much ease as I could, to all but the goats who nothing troubles, except the moment of slaughter. One of the cows was with calf and would need to lay a place apart. The pony looked like it wanted to bound into the sea rather than drown with the rest of us. When I saw the feed, I knew I would not keep these animals alive for so long, whatever the seas. Yardsley too, feared for his plant life.

'There is no light down here, and it is damp, all the soil is claggy without much drainage. On deck, the salt wind will tear them to shreds. Wind stresses a plant you know and I'm going to need some grit from somewhere, and there's something else.'

'You're going to tell me that plants can't swim?'

'I'm telling you I don't know what half of them are. There's cabbages, pear, apple, onion, radishes.'

'Who would think to bring radishes from one end of the earth to the other?'

'There's other plants I don't know at all. I was a gardener. I grew flowers for families that didn't need to grow food. I'm good with roses, but there's none here.'

'That's a shame.'

'What is?' he asked.

'Supposing there's no roses when we get there. Imagine living without roses.'

Henry Dodd spent most of his time with Yardsley, having him run up-and-down between decks providing one plant with light another with shelter. Yardsley collected water from rain, hail, and snow and drank barely any himself. Dodd got bones from the cook and ground them down to meal to add to the soil. Peelings he fermented into a liquid feed. We learnt that Henry Dodd was the commodore's servant and gardener, an important man all the same.

The crew barely spoke a word to us the six long weeks to Botany Bay. The day we went down to their quarters, two hammocks were thrown at us and we lashed them up where we could. There was amongst them many languages and arguments, some having joined the ship at The Cape, some having been captured after deserting. On deck, there was never a crossed word, for the commodore of the whole fleet, Captain Phillip was aboard. Below, it was a different matter.

'Ships don't come back from these waters, the only ships that venture this far are desperate whalers ...'

'The ocean can't be read, it fights itself where cold water meets the warm ...'

'You don't know what you're talking about,' a Dutchman said. 'Plenty of Dutch sailors have come and gone from these waters. Why do you suppose it's called New Holland?'

'And have you ever been there?'

'There's nothing to be frightened of,' said the Dutchman.

No-one had been there, but sailors do not admit to fear. Fear on a voyage is like scurvy, it is for people who cling to the land. Perhaps they wouldn't speak to us because we were not sailors, as much as because we were convicts, but what I knew to be true was that not even the commodore had been to New Holland before, or had even been in the great Southern Ocean. Fear vented itself in bad tempers amongst officers and men. The commodore himself, whenever I saw him stroll the main deck with his greyhounds, he never looked on the swollen waters, but was always thinking on some other matter. Marines and crew bickered like stoats, disobeying orders, for which they were lashed. As the weather worsened, the rigging moaned under sleet and snow, the crew tarred their shirts so they wouldn't soak, and bid us to do the same. There were days when no other ships were in sight and the word went about that some had sunk. The greyhounds had the run of the ship and many wanted them over the side, a seaman kicked the pony and Dodd saw to it that he was flogged, but with one stroke only, for the shame of it, saying to me, 'A man that is cruel to animals is a weak man, the type that would beat women and children.'

I sat with the cow the night its calf was born, and watched an officer lie on his back noting the heavens in a journal. The calf was weak but so was its mother, and there was precious little milk. I sat with the calf for three more nights until it died. It was the same number of days and nights Susanna and me had sat with our first-born, Elizabeth, Susanna's milk and rose-syrup on our fingers. Just like then, the third night turned deathly cold. After little Elizabeth died, we would not move her for two days. Susanna thought it might be her last child at her age. I met the doctor on the lane, the doctor who did not come to poor people like us, he tipped his hat. When a rich woman loses a child it is a calamity felt by all in the village; when a poor woman does it is to be expected and borne.

The calf was eaten and its bones ground-up for meal. Henry Dodd came over to comfort me and I told him I thought the cow would give-up as well now.

'All things want to live,' he said.

'But they must have a land to live on. A place that is right for them.'

When we finally sighted our Mount Ararat, it had a snowy cap but no rainbow. We watched the coastline to see what the land held for us. It seemed, from a distance, not infertile. As we pushed on a wind arose to force us away and a corporal was swept into the tumult. Clothed as he was, he would have sunk had not the seaman who had kicked the pony tied a rope to himself and gone into the hurling waves to bring him back. After two weeks of fighting it, the headwind died and we drifted into Botany Bay, the livestock that had survived craving the earth.

I saw the New Holland natives for the first time and I was afeared and excited. They stood on the cliff tops, at the beach top, the sun behind them, coal black statues against the silken sky. As we closed in, I could see they were naked bar their beards and that they held spears, some stabbing them at the air making their purpose plain. I saw about the land beyond the beach an abundance of birds, large, brightly-coloured, one that sounded like a lamb. It was near noon in the middle of January but the deck was hot underfoot. When the ship anchored, all were told to go below. The crew shouted at the natives and the bosun shut them up.

'Do you think they'll be fighting?' asked Yardsley, 'with the natives?'

'Wouldn't be much of a fight. They have their spears and the redcoats have their muskets,' I said.

'But they have the numbers. And I wouldn't mind if a native stuck a marine or two, would you?' he asked.

It was I agreed a bloody and pleasing thought. Out of a porthole, I saw a cockatoo for the first time and was possessed by its shell white feathers, its buttercup hat. I thought I would give what feed and water was left to the livestock and was granted permission. On deck a small boat was being untethered, the officer with the journal, the commodore and two marines were standing by. After eight months at sea, all on board were threadbare, but one of the marines had polished his brass and silverware for this occasion. He was a Goliath, the sun bobbing off him as he moved. I loathe redcoats. They are mostly cruel, birdbrain men, ruling with rifle butt and blade, who have starved me and flogged me, but I did fear for them having to land on that beach. They went down the ladder and I watched a native boy run down the beach making to launch his spear. He was showing-off to the others, but there would be killing for sure. The Goliath raised his head at the ladder top, 'You. You're needed in the boat.'

I had hold of a pig and I didn't let it go. He came onto the deck and put his hand on the hilt of his sword.

'Move I say!'

I had to take the oars and had my back to the beach. I watched the face of the officer, if he was to flinch so would I. The commodore put a hand on my shoulder.

'This will do. Raise oars.'

We were a little out, with rocks between us and the beach. Goliath ordered me again, 'You, in the water.'

I was up to my knees, surf rolling in and then he climbed on my back, pressing me down, legs dangling either side. I walked across the rocks like a drunk, heaved him onto the sand. The blacks were shouting ever louder, so I smartly went back and forward to carry the commodore and the other officer. I stood behind the three of them as they faced the natives. I hadn't asked to come there, we weren't wanted, and I wasn't fighting anyone for the right to be a slave in a land hotter than hell. The commodore stepped forward, put out an arm for the others not to follow. He walked slowly towards the line of natives at the head of the beach, just in front of trees, still in leaf. A man, strong looking, came down to meet him half-way. The commodore showed him his palms, removed his hat, and bowed. Without a word from either, the native threw down his spear and then the others behind him did the same. They all stood, quite still and silent. The commodore cupped his hands and made as if to drink, and he did this again until the chief native smiled and pointed down the beach where in the distance we could see others.

I carried the three of them back to the boat and rowed them there. Carted them once more onto the land they would lay claim to. Me, a farmhand, someone who was shooed off the fields of England like a jackdaw, who could be starved, whipped or hanged on the word of a superior, whose name was of no matter to the man on his back, my feet were the first on that land. On the second beach, the natives did not brandish their spears. We walked among them, for they were mostly women. They showed the commodore where the stream was, he gave them some coloured beads in return.

CHAPTER 13

The Sacred Place

I was lying under the boat with Williams. McIntyre and Scottish Jack were under canvas. We'd propped up the hull with a few rocks to lay our legs outside. We lay between sealskins. The nights were dwindling, the days not yet full-grown. It had been more than a week since the skins were taken, or since McIntyre stated they were. But if Maoris had come and taken them, why had they not come for us as well? They were fearless fighters, not London sneak-thieves. The answer I decided was because the thief was McIntyre. McIntyre and Scottish Jack working together no doubt. They had secreted the skins away somewhere because McIntyre had told Scottish Jack that me and Williams were planning to do the same. As the month came to an end, he would convince Scottish Jack to help him cut our throats, by claiming that we planned to do the same to them. McIntyre was Lucifer, turning man against man.

'John, do you really think someone came and took those skins?'

'Could be.'

'You know what I think? I think McIntyre has put them to one side somewhere. And that he has plans for the rest of the skins, and us.'

For once, his reply came directly.

'Then we should kill them both before Evans comes back.'

I looked over at John and watched him drawing on the bottom of the boat with his finger.

At first light I slid away and walked to the bay that McIntyre and Scottish Jack had been working. Sunrise was streaked by cloud and the water wore a thickness. I wasn't sure what I was looking for. I didn't expect to see a few hundred skins piled between the dunes. I reckoned they would have buried them in a pit, and marked the place with stone. More than likely the place would be closer to where Evans was to meet us, not the far end of the bay. I came across a rough circle of stones and wondered at its meaning, but decided that was where nature had placed them. I walked into the dunes where there were fewer stones and thought, if I saw any at all, they could have been put there as a marker. I passed through them and came to a clearing, where at its centre was a small stone pillar. Could they have both lifted it? I ran my fingers over it and could feel it had been cut, in ancient times I thought. Perhaps it marked a grave. I climbed the hillock at the back of the bay, and was sure again, the island was a place of solitude. A great anvil of cloud in the sky was blackening. A wind was mustering, I could smell the rain. We were going to be beset by a storm and the missing sealskins were still on the island.

At the camp McIntyre was frying fish.

'You want me to put a piece in the pan for you Ruse?' he asked.

'I want you to tell me where the skins are,' I replied.

He straightened up and looked me in the eye.

'You heard what we said. We spent three days round the corner, and when we came back, they were gone.'

'Did you see anyone?'

'No, did you? Maybe they came at night.'

He began to eat his fish, offered me some.

'Maybe they didn't come at all. Maybe you have them hidden and plan to take the rest and rid yourselves of me and Williams,' I said.

'You know Ruse, me and Jack were just saying the same thing last night. That you two had hidden the skins in your cave down there, and you figured that all four of us wouldn't be leaving the island.'

'Listen to me,' said Scottish Jack. 'Those skins are gone. We have another two weeks before Evans comes for us, and who knows how many more months we'll be out hunting after that. We can't be at each others' throats.'

The wind began to spray us all with sand so we took shelter in the dunes.

'Where are we hunting next?' asked Jack.

'We stay hereabouts,' I said. 'I'm not leaving what we've got. Evans won't be happy when we tell him how many we've already lost.'

The seals were coming back to the beach where we'd begun to kill them. They always do. They don't have a memory of bloodshed, only where they must lie. Before long though, the storm was such that we couldn't work and we had to cower back down in the dunes. Even worse than the rain were the winds and the prospect of waves taking us away. We could not stand in it, we could not sleep. We buried the skins we had and fled inland, through the marsh to the trees at the centre of the island. Amid the trees, there was some shelter, some peace from the fury, and it cured us of our quarrelling.

'This is not the time of year for storms, not like this,' said Scottish Jack.

'I know,' I said, 'seems this island has us cursed.'

The mutton-birds had their burrows, what other birds there were were roosting in the trees. We had a sheet of canvas to cover the four of us. Through the night, we could hear the passion of the waves a mile or two away, and I wondered if they would swallow the whole island. Scottish Jack was on his feet at dawn. I followed him out the other side of the woods. He was standing in a clearing, with a stone pillar at its centre, this time with a low wall all around.

'This is a sacred place,' he said. 'It's where people say farewell to the dead. We shouldn't be here, the spirits won't like it.'

'Are people buried here?' I asked.

'Spirits are here. We are on their ground. We have to go.'

'We can't go until the storm has ended,' I said. 'This is the only shelter.'

Scottish Jack looked-up at the bobbing tree tops, looked at the long grass beyond the clearing, gripping the ground.

'I'd rather face the storm,' he said. 'Restless spirits take the spirits of the living.'

'And how do they do that?' I asked.

'They guide them towards death. We do the rest ourselves.'

He turned, began to walk back.

'We should never have come.'

He walked past McIntyre and Williams, recently arisen. McIntyre watched Jack walk out of the woods and meet the wind.

'Where's he off to?'

'The dunes, I think. He says there are spirits here.'

'Jesus.'

'He looked scared. But I'm not going after him, and neither is anyone else.'

'Damn right Ruse. He's nothing but a lazy bastard.'

We stayed a second night. Williams spent the day carving an image of a boy from a piece of wood. Whenever McIntyre asked him to get more firewood, Williams didn't answer. After the third occasion, McIntyre snatched the carving and threw it on the fire. Williams didn't seize it from the flames. He watched it burn instead.

When we returned to the bay in the morning and we got near the dunes we could see our lifeboat, not where we had left it but some yards back. I supposed Jack had dragged it back for shelter. But even before we reached it, Williams picked up a piece of the hull from the ground and began looking for others. The boat was broken, smashed below the water line. There was no Scottish Jack. I ran to the place where we had buried the skins; they were still there. Then we saw him, further down the beach, with driftwood under his arm. He waved at us merrily, whilst we were fretful of our situation.

'Jack, what happened to the boat?'

'I think it must have been damaged by the storm.'

CHAPTER 14

New Albion

New Holland, 1788

How New Holland first seemed and how it came to pass was not the same. That first day at Botany Bay the natives were gentle, welcoming, as was the sun. From beyond, the land looked fertile. Once we dug-in up the coast at the cove we found the soil to be meagre, rocky, and unfruitful. I wondered at how the trees found any nourishment, at their brittle burned bark, their ground-hard wood. The grass so harsh and sour, hardy sheep could not live on it. We were put to work clearing the land of trees and shrubs the day we arrived in Port Jackson, a harbour many times the size of Plymouth and London put together. The governor had in his mind a great city, a New Jerusalem, with citizens taken with new hearts and minds. We were to build a town, a country, to replace the gaols and gallows of England.

It was January and I believed it to be winter, though my skin burned red as we grubbed-up roots and broke our tools on gum and cabbage trunks. I never saw New Holland as anything but an unnatural place, always compared to Cornwall and wanting. I missed the curling, sunken lanes, the bluebell slopes, my moss-walls. The trees were far apart for the want of soil and water, the earth red or burned black. It was a half-starved ghost of a forest that once was. At first, I could only take to the land where it reminded me of England, but after a while I began to see the brightness of the light on the small, pale, leaves, how sound is never buried in a New Holland wood, but bounces off the naked trees. The abundance of the stone-coloured creatures on the ground and the many coloured birds of the sky. Even as I stood amidst the bone-coloured trees, hurt by hunger, I would rejoice at God's earth.

When we men were first put ashore, many were idle for weeks. There were not enough tools for all to work, there was no industry to attend to, there was little desire for toil. Officers and convicts alike were dumbfounded by the queerness of the land they had come to, and after such a great voyage many were taken with bouts of melancholy. First, I and others had to clear land for livestock pens, then day-after-day, endless hacking away for tents and huts. Work was a stranger to many convicts, their minds would stray elsewhere right after they were handed the hoe. Charles Peat took to giving one and all instructions, like a squire who had long been farming in New Holland. *Why don't you use that to lever those rocks over there ... dig at that tree from one side, then push it from the other ... Worry not, that spider won't harm you.* John Williams was a fine worker. He worked doggedly at his own pace only stopping when Peat interrupted him. The boy Barrett, the *Mercury* man from the hulk who cut love tokens, was the idlest labourer I ever met. Had I not known his guile I would've had him down as an idiot. Coining and thieving were his crafts, and he was hard pressed to make use of them at the cove. Will Bryant had talked his way into fishing duties. First day, they threw a seine right across the cove. He'd never seen a catch like it.

'Eels, rays, carp, cat-fish, flounders, herrings, fish I don't know, brightly coloured, there must have been a hundred variety, and there was a shark there. The natives they came down and were jumping and dancing, I filled a canoe for one. Me and Mary, we won't starve if they let me fish, Ruse.'

I thought, if they let me farm, I might. Those that knew trades were put to them, the brickmaster, the blacksmith, the carpenters. Redcoats went about their business of shooting birds, bats, kangaroos and all else, if only for a closer look at them, or for an officer to draw in his journal.

Sometimes the natives would come to the edge of the woods as we cut them down. An old man put his hand on a cabbage tree as me and Williams were hacking at it. He talked in his strange language, I think about the tree, or perhaps to the tree, since it was that he looked upon. He placed his fingers in some notches cut into the bark. He had a beard down to his frail chest, the flesh hung off his bones, his hair tied-up above his head, pipe clay on his face. Behind him a young man carrying a spear, behind him a woman with a child, all entirely naked. The child had yellow feathers in his hair, the bonniest boy I'd seen since my son Richard five years before. Charles Peat stepped forward, acting like a spokesman for the fleet.

'Charles ... I am Charles,' his palm on his breast. 'We are going to build a house with the tree,' he drew a house in the air, 'and you can come inside the house and sit in it. With us.'

'Waroo, waroo,' said the old man, pointing to the sea.

The tree went to the sawpit and as we carried it I noticed that the notches went all along either side of the trunk. The natives had a playfulness that we had forgotten, they could copy our words better than we theirs. Williams greeted the same family whenever he could and would exchange words with them, *yannadah* for moon, *boorawa* for sky. They were good-natured people, patient and forgiving, more so than any Cornishmen would have been, had they arrived at Plymouth and started tearing down the woods.

Late one afternoon, after a week of clearing, tents were pitched and the women were brought on shore. Men watched as the boats ferried them closer. Between our tents and theirs was a line of marines and an acre of ground, and both were needed. The women knew that there would be hundreds of pairs of eyes upon them, and most seemed to have prepared themselves as best as they could. I could tell, even from a distance, that many were frightened. As soon as they set foot on the cove men stood and began shouting names and profanities. Some tried to push past the redcoats, who held them back, I reckoned only because they wanted to get there before them. Will Bryant shinned up a tree to look for Mary from Fowey, the girl he had taken to on the hulk.

'Can you see her Will?'

'No I can't. She will have the child with her. I'll kill any man that touches either of them.'

Sailors had come ashore behind the women, carrying rum, which they meant to bargain their way to the women with. Will jumped down from the tree, rolling on the ground, running before he could stand, towards the line of redcoats.

'You need to let me through, that's my woman, the one with the child.'

'No-one gets through. Governor's orders,' snapped the redcoat.

'I need to protect her. She's only just given birth.'

'She's your wife?' asked the redcoat.

'We are promised to one another.'

'If you were married, you'd have your own tent, wouldn't yer?' The redcoat pushed Will Bryant back.

Will Bryant was about to strike him, I placed my hand on his shoulder.

'Other women will protect her Will. Her and the child.'

'Easier to protect a lamb from wolves,' he said.

Some of the sailors had outflanked the marines, and women were swigging from jugs. As darkness closed in bats the size of ducks that hung in the trees turned the corners of the sky black. The sound of women's laughter, and then screams, could be heard from one end of the cove to the other. It goaded the men and, all at once, they charged through the darkness and through the redcoats, who were either too slow to stop them or running with them at the women. Will sprinted with the pack, knocking over the marine that had stopped him before, with me and Williams following.

'Mary! Mary Broad ... it's Will,' he shouted.

Men lifted women off their feet, carried them away, some with the women laughing, some with them screaming and fighting. Men fought each other, two, three at a time over a woman. Redcoats demanded first pickings. Some men and women sat and talked to one another, like it was any other evening in Launceston. The officers were nowhere to be seen.

'Will, over here!'

Mary crawled out of a tent with her infant. Will took her by the arm and led her away into the woods behind the camp. She walked awkwardly, as she always did. The four of us sat there with the child, watching the scene below us. She had folded Charlotte into a cloth, calling her after the transport ship she was born on. The father of the child, she never did say. When Will took Charlotte to nurse her, Mary would have her back straight away, for she was always in mortal fear for her.

'They have taken too many men here and not enough women, that's a recipe for war,' said Mary.

New Holland is more alive in the dark. It begins with the crickets, then the movement of bats. In the woods, you can hear the scuttering of creatures before your feet, there are pairs of red eyes, close to the ground. The birds, who do not have songs but only strange calls, one like a wheel in need of oil, mark the coming of darkness. But that night, there was little to be heard. Then the heat turned into fire. Lightning divided the sky, striking a tree which turned to flame. Though the rain was a torrent, it could not put out the fire. Hogs and sheep were found the next day, made black by a bolt. Lightning showed-up men and women, laying together in the washed away earth.

Next morning, all the convicts, were made to sit on the beach, surrounded on all sides by marines. The commodore and his officers came to the front. Dawes was there and also Captain Tench from the hulk. The commodore was made governor of New Holland with the powers of a king, and he spoke on how he was going to rule his kingdom. Any man seen near a women's tent would be shot. Anyone stealing food would be hanged. Anyone harming the natives would be flogged, hanged if they killed them. The rules applied to marines and convicts alike, as did the rations. Convicts who wouldn't work wouldn't eat. There was nowhere to escape to but the wilderness. He spoke about us all beginning again, building a fine town, leading good lives. That he had once intended to call this place New Albion, but had decided to call it Sydney after a Lord in England, but it would be a new country all the same. Then Tench shouted 'God Save the King!' and so did we. The redcoats fired a round into the air, a host of parakeets scattered and cried.

In the tents at night, men talked about how they could not and would not live on rations, how they would escape to China, how they would not work, and how they would take native women whenever they got the chance. That's when I first met McIntyre, an Irishman and a *Mercury* man.

'Those native women. Some of them don't belong to anyone. I mean, they don't have men,' he said.

'They have fathers,' said Peat, 'and I think the governor's idea is to win them over.'

'I'll be winning the women over all right. Besides, who they gonna tell?' said McIntyre.

'Well when they get the pox from you, someone will know,' said Barrett. 'Listen, he said, 'I heard there's French ships back at that first bay we were in, and it ain't far to walk there. Keep going south I'm told.'

Peat was suddenly interested.

'And what else did you hear?'

'Well they ain't brought convicts so they won't be staying.'

'And which way's south?' asked Peat.

I was in the queue for my rations of beef and pease when Captain Tench and Henry Dodd, the governor's servant from the *Supply*, came up to me. Tench had the same air about him, acting like he was somewhere else, on a stroll after church, glancing at the convicts like they were goods at a market.

'I do believe you two know each other,' he said.

'We do,' said Dodd. 'Are you well, James Ruse?'

'I am sir.'

Dodd's face was redder than anyone's I'd seen at the cove. His skin had taken badly to the sun and he had made a kind of wicker hat from tree bark. Like the rest of us, he was thinning as well.

'Do you know where Yardsley is, the gardener?' he asked.

'He's in that tent over there sir,' I said.

Yardsley like Dodd was a Shropshire man, and both gardeners.

'Good. What are the men you've been working with like, as workers?'

'No better or worse than any convicts I reckon?'

'Any farmers among them?' he asked.

'None. But Williams is as good a grafter as any farmhand I saw.'

Then Tench explained what I had already worked-out for myself.

'Mr Dodd here is going to create a farm to feed the settlement. You and your men are going to work on it.'

'Where's it to be,' I asked.

Tench pointed behind him.

'The next cove to the east.'

We started the same day, beginning at the head of the cove, rather than up from the beach. It meant the party walked deep into the woods which we were fretful about. Dodd refused Tench's offer of a marine escort saying, 'This is our new home, and I do not want to always live with soldiers about me.'

We came to a natural clearing, Dodd thrust a spade into the ground. 'Here!' he cried.

He had to wait for Barrett and Peat, to catch up. Each of us was carrying a tool or a length of rope. Two carried barrels of water. The ground had begun to slope away from the head, and we could no longer see the sea behind us.

'This is where we will begin the settlement farm. Clearing towards the beach. We plant as we clear. There are nearly a thousand souls depending on the success of this farm. Depending on us, our toil. The clearing of the ground must be thorough, you are not clearing for tents but for seed. Leave no roots behind.'

He sent a man off to find a stream, telling him to mark his path on every fourth tree with a hatchet so he knew his way back. Then he paced out the width of the farm and hammered two stakes into the ground. There were fifteen or so of us, and he split the group in two, and told us to work towards one another, and meet in the middle. Like any forced labour, men did not want to do it, but they were unsure what would happen to them if they refused. Could Dodd order a flogging? Though Dodd wouldn't say himself, I told one or two he was the governor's servant. When Barrett stopped and sat down after no time at all, Dodd went over and spoke like a father to a son.

'The way to work in this heat, is to work slowly son. You have to understand that what you are doing is making the first ever farm on this land. It is a wonderful thing we are doing, to make a land fertile.'

Then he lifted Barrett to his feet.

'You are not a slave my boy, you are a farmer.'

For a few minutes, Barrett got about his work like a Trojan. He hacked away at a root, cursing it, and held it up like a trophy once he'd got it out of the ground.

'Mr Dodd, sir, look. Got it out.'

Then he spotted Peat at the water barrel, drinking from a ladle and went over. Dodd called them back to work, 'You cannot take water whenever you like, there will be a set time when we all drink.'

Barrett nodded to Peat and they both scurried into the woods, going south. Mr Dodd did not give chase, nor did he speak of it. Nor was he deterred. There were plenty more convicts and we were less important than the farm. McIntyre worked but became more bad-tempered with every minute. When we did stop for water, Dodd spoke only about the soil.

'Thankfully we have the manure, from our livestock. What we don't have is time. I'd like to give the ground a year or two, but we can't.'

'Where we come across ashes we should dig them in, grass as well,' I said. 'But what we need most of all is a flood plain.'

'The governor has found a substantial river, but no plain.'

The old native man was at the edge of the clearing, his hand on a tree once more. Dodd rose and offered him water, which he was grateful for. Behind, the younger man, the woman and child. They drank and smiled. McIntyre was on his feet and bothering the woman in no time. Mr Dodd gave them a hatchet; they gave him a spear and went on their way. Somewhere along the journey back to the cove, McIntyre and another convict slipped away into the woods. There was a muster when we got back and they were noted missing. Only McIntyre came back, late at night, without his shirt, bloodied and scratched.

In the morning, Tench came to the tent and took him away. The governor had a court sitting where men were tried and sentenced and witnesses called, just for cracking another convict or giving some lip to an officer. At first the governor exiled men to an island in the harbour, but then it was back to hanging and flogging, same as England. McIntyre was given fifty lashes and we were all lined-up to watch. Floggings in New Holland draw the flies, the cockroaches that take pieces of a man's back away when it's flicked off by the cat. When we went off to the farm, Tench insisted on three marines going with us, with orders to shoot at any convict that ran into the woods. One of the marines was Piggott from the hulk. Almost all his teeth had gone and his nose was peeling like an onion. I was surprised he had survived the journey.

'Here we are again Ruse. You always said how you wanted to work outside. You got your chance now, haven't you?'

Piggott shot at a cockatoo and Dodd scolded him for it, to which Piggott told him, 'You ain't no officer to me. I give these to the surgeon and he paints them.'

Almost at the same time that they had run away the day before, Peat and Barrett came walking back into the clearing. They looked like they had been walking ever since they left. Peat staggered up to Mr Dodd.

'We were lost all night sir, and are glad that we are back with you again. I wonder, may we have some water?'

Dodd took them over to the barrel, a native's lance flew down, pinning Piggott to the tree he was leaning against. He breathed in once then died with his eyes open, the lance still quivering. A redcoat knelt and fired-up, shooting a native man high up in a cabbage tree. He dropped to the ground. When we went to him, he was either dead or insensible. The redcoat who had shot him was excited, breathing quickly. I looked-up the trunk of the great tree and saw the notches the native must have cut to climb it.

CHAPTER 15

The Stony Ground

William Bryant and Mary Broad were married along with four other couples all standing on the grass outside the reverend's tent on a Sunday. I was one that bore witness. The reverend was always occupied with marriages, christenings, and burials. There was no church, no desire to build one. The coiner Barrett had fashioned a ring from a shell for Will to give to Mary. Will gave Barrett some fish in return, which Barrett exchanged with someone else for some pease. Standing there listening to them take their vows, I realised there were more people at this wedding than at my own. Susanna hadn't yet begun to show, yet my father was too good to come. In New Holland, no-one is too good for anyone. Susanna looked beautiful that day, the most beautiful she ever was. Her hair so thick and soft I wanted to sleep on it. She had on a family dress, and looked like a lady. And she looked relieved. But Mary, Mary with her base-born child Charlotte, named after a transport ship, ragged and grubby Mary and Will, were more delighted than we were, and frightened of no-one.

Women had come to have the pick of men in the camp. The governor had had them protected and the marines could not possess them at their will anymore. They had their own rations and none had to beg or offer favours. One marine struck another for speaking to a friend of Mary's, because he had owned her on the voyage. But it was different in the camp and he was lashed for that. Some women wanted marriage, some liked to play from one man to another, stay in the women's camp. Mary and Will, they had a hut near me. We built them ourselves in what Dodd was calling Farm Cove. There, we were away from most of the other convicts and from the redcoats. The huts we made of wattle and daub and I had to show Will. We were short of dung because it was needed for manure and our walls crumbled with the rain, but most of the timber that was cut was used for the officer's houses and the barracks. Likewise, we found that clay roofs fell in and that a thatch of gum rushes held-up, but didn't keep out the water. We puddled out the clay for the floor and our windows were a lattice of twigs. They were hovels, no better or worse than a labourer's in Cornwall. I shared a hut with Williams who spent little time in it and made his midden by the door. I doubted he had lived in a house much at all. He liked to wander the woods and would try and speak with the natives, brought them in his hut out of the rain. He told me they called Farm Cove, *Goo-ga-roo.*

Will Bryant fished across the harbour in a cutter. He was supposed to hand over all of the catch but he had a way of holding some back for himself, and sometimes for me and Williams. No officer or marine could fish or sail like him. In truth, the redcoats couldn't do much in the way of work apart from threaten and flog. The ships that had brought us were going home with the ship's carpenters and sailmakers. Few convicts knew a trade, people died from ignorance. Those that knew something were made the overseers and one day Dodd came to me and asked, 'This farm you had. You had men labouring for you?'

'I did. I had a few.'

'Well then, you're overseer on the farm.'

'Alright then,' I said to him, 'but the first thing is I want rid of Barrett.'

'He's young, he needs to learn,' he said.

'He's past learning. He has a convict's mind. He don't think in seasons, about feeding people, he's watching and waiting until he can steal what's grown.'

Barrett was put on collecting oyster shells with the women to give to the brickmaster to make lime. He was fleered at for it, but didn't mind.

I stood behind Dodd as he bent double and pulled out a shoot from the crumbly earth. He looked at the faintest of roots. I'd seen stronger spider legs.

'I do wonder if the seeds got overheated on the voyage,' he said.

'It's not the seeds,' I said. 'It's the soil and it's the heat here.'

I had given up toadying to him, since I had broken my back clearing land that did not want a farm.

'The heat has drawn out a stem that's too long, and the roots cannot grip the earth because it's so dry.'

We had cleared and planted fifteen acres with wheat and corn and some vegetables. The vegetables stood a better chance because they were underground. But we would not feed more than a few hundred for five minutes, even if there was a harvest.

Dodd dusted his hands and faced me.

'I want them watering today,' he said.

'We need to compost the grass, anything that'll feed it.'

He didn't argue. He was from Shropshire, I had farmed in Cornwall. It wasn't as bad as New Holland, but it wasn't generous. The work party arrived from Sydney Cove. They were spent before they started. McIntyre was among them and he grumbled, then said the farm workers ought to eat more than the rest. They lined-up, looking to me. I gave out orders, my own voice sounding strange to me again.

'We need two pits dug, grass and seaweed collected,' I said. 'Then we fill the pits.'

'Then what?' asked McIntyre.

'Then we wait.'

Part of me thought, I might as well tell them to go hunting with the natives. Williams knew this but said nothing. I had told him more than once that this was sheep-farming land, if only we had the right grass. But many of the sheep had gone astray, been taken by the natives, or had died on the diet. If the potatoes could have run off, they would have. John Williams worked on, worked hard for me. Come darkness, me and him would have to chase off the vermin, creatures that would eat a scarecrow. Williams had a spear given to him by a native. He would run round the acres throwing it at anything and nothing, and it worried me that one night he might mistake me for a kangaroo.

One day after work, early in that first year, we all had to go to the main camp and stand between the men and women's tents. I thought it was a muster, because some men had run away. We were surrounded by redcoats, with only one officer to look at beneath a tree. Then the reverend came walking toward us, leading Barrett, his hands tied behind him, and two other men. The reverend was reading aloud. They got to the front and the officer spoke to us all.

'These men are condemned to death for stealing from the Government stores. Let this be a lesson to you all. Carry on.'

A young marine, his uniform too big, ran rattling over to him, clutching a piece of paper.

'From the governor, sir.'

The officer read it and nodded, 'Take these two away.'

The lad grabbed the shirts of the other two and half-dragged them back to where they'd come from. Barrett watched them go and looked at the officer. A ladder was brought to the tree behind them, a fig tree. A rope with a noose was flung over the lowest branch. There was not a sound amongst the hundreds of us that were made to watch this. Barrett was calm, calmer than I was. He asked the officer something. The officer nodded, hands behind his back. Barrett stepped forward and was embraced by a man I know to be Robert Sidaway, a Londoner. Then he climbed the ladder, a marine advanced and tightened the rope around his neck, then jumped down. It was going to be a convict who had to pull the ladder away. The reverend, sweat running down his face, finished reading from *The Burial of the Dead*, 'I am the resurrection and the life, saith the Lord, he that believeth in me, though he were dead, yet shall he live, and whosoever liveth and believeth in me, shall never die.'

Barrett was still very much alive. The convict Nichols put both hands on the ladder, looked-up at Barrett, who spoke to us all.

'I've led a very wicked life,' he said. 'This is how it must end for me. Take heed of what the major says.'

I closed my eyes, but heard nothing. When I opened them again, Nichols' hands were fast on the ladder. The major ordered, 'Pull the ladder away.'

Nichols looked at the major as if he hadn't heard him right.

'The ladder man, hang him!'

The hangman stared into the face of the man he had to hang. He looked to the major, begging a reprieve.

'Private, take aim at Nichols,' ordered the major. 'Nichols, if you don't pull the ladder from under the prisoner, you will be shot, and then I'll do it myself.'

The musket couldn't have been more than a yard from Nichols' head. Still he wouldn't pull the ladder.

'On the count of three Nichols, pull the ladder. One, two ...'

There was a moment's cry from Barrett, as a child screams for his mother, then he was turned-off, jerking twice or thrice. As we filed away, I saw Charles Peat. His face was as white as poor Barrett's. They left his body hanging until dark, buried it near the tree, the grave not marked. That night, hail fell heavily from the sky, washing him from his grave, washing away wheat shoots on the farm.

As we sunk into the middle of the year I began to believe that the land did not want our presence, for man cannot live everywhere. When you try to farm, the land will tell you how you must live, what you may grow and eat, and there was good reason why the natives of New Holland were not farmers. Vegetables were growing, corn we knew there would be some come harvest, wheat, I knew would fail. Each convict had a kitchen garden of his own, though many had no idea how to tend it, or else had no strength come Sunday. Some would come at night to Farm Cove to steal potatoes and turnips, and Williams and me, we had to fend them off, as well as the vermin and the natives. All the ships went from the harbour, one took convicts to an island many miles east to try and plant there. Some marines said the settlement was to be abandoned; that a ship would soon be taking them home, leaving us to face the natives alone. Fear and hunger drove people to the edge of their minds. As the weekly ration was cut, by the fourth or fifth day people had eaten everything they had, and stole to stay alive or else died. A man I know, a tin miner in England and hardy, lay down on the farm as the life ran out of him. I closed his sunken eyes with my hands. One of his mates told me he knew he was selling some of his rations to marines for coin, so that he might one day buy his passage back to England.

People stole without fear or much reason, with the certainty they would be flogged at the triangle or the tree. Clothes, plates, blankets, nothing could be left in huts or tents. Daley, a strange man, broke-up a brass buckle, mixed it with earth, and showed a handful to Tench, saying he had found gold in the woods up-river. Maybe he was a hoping for a reward of rations. He had Tench and some redcoats rowing for a day-and-a-half, until he confessed he had made fools of them, for which he was flogged. Not long from the triangle, he stole another convict's clothes and peached from the fatal tree on the woman he had sold them to. She had her head shaven and was made to wear a smock with *RSG* sewn on to it, *Receiver of Stolen Goods*.

But hunger doesn't mind shame and convicts took to peaching and making witness to the court that met every day, doling out punishments ever more savage for matters ever smaller. But nothing did deter. Women were whipped through the camp at the tail end of a cart for something said. A boy, eighteen at most, was dragged straight from court to the fatal tree, there hanged for stealing sugar and bread. His fellows in the crime were tied to the tree and flogged whilst he hung above them. The governor's dreams of Jerusalem ended on the branch of that tree, and with the transporting of men to islands out in the harbour who had already been transported across the world. Put men where you want, they will always sin. We were made so since we were driven from Eden, and our fleet full of sinners had wound its way to a new Eden, like the serpent it was.

One Sunday, Captain Tench and two privates came to Farm Cove and looked in Will and Mary's hut. They found three fish. They looked in mine and Williams' and found nothing they wanted. Will Bryant was sentenced to a hundred lashes for keeping back the fish. Dodd allowed me to go with Mary to stand by him, and we stood where he could see us, while they flogged him. Alongside us was James Martin, the Irishman from the hulk, who was now fishing with Bryant. Will never buckled under the lash whilst natives howled from behind the trees. One, a woman, came forward and swung a stick at the corporal laying-on. She was pushed back at bayonet point. Bryant walked away from the triangle as upright as he had walked there. On the way back to our huts, he rested his arms on me and Mary.

'How did they know James, how did they know?'

'Someone peached. That's how. One of the work party must have smelt the fish. They'll be giving food to people who give names.'

Back at his hut, Mary had willow bark for him to chew and leaves for his back.

'I'm not staying. This ain't Plymouth, we can go, we can run,' he said.

'To where though? This is a wilderness unending.'

He hadn't an answer, yet.

'I caught that fish. They won't let me live by my own hand.'

'We don't have much more than a year, do we,' I said. 'Then our seven will be up. Four on the hulk, a year to get here.'

Bryant, a man who had just taken a hundred lashes, laughed at me.

'Tench or someone, they're going to come-up and say, "James Ruse, your ship awaits," are they?'

Mary, her fingers all bloodied from Will's cuts, looked at me staunchly.

'You trust them all you want James,' she said, 'but we ain't got time for that. They'll most likely hang him in less than a year.'

Whatever plans he had about escape, Mary had them as well.

As spring was coming to England, it freshened in New Holland. Winds picked-up, swallows, a dab of red on their necks, gathered and left; days shortened. It was autumn and I understood that nature there was in reverse. Leaves fell and bark peeled but I much missed the richness of England's autumn, the crab apples, the over-ripe rosehips. Come the king's birthday there was a day free from labour for us all. We were each given a half-pint of rum, canons were fired to salute him, bonfires were lit, two men to be executed were pardoned. Yet we were so far from him, and it was said he had gone mad. Were we really his people anymore?

There was a harvest of corn, as good as any I had seen, but the wheat was only good for seed. Barley and other seeds had rotted in the ground. Dodd and I looked out across the twenty acres, too much of it bare.

'We shall have to plant again,' he said.

'Well then, we will be in the ground ourselves by the time it comes,' I said.

I got to my knees and scratched the earth a little, held the crawling thing, the size of an almond, between my fingers. '

'The ground is full of weevils, sir.'

McIntyre told us that sailors had let it be known that the *Sirius* was being stripped-out to sail to The Cape for food.

'And they are going via The Horn. Be lucky if they make it,' he said, as if he wished us all to starve, just to see the look on an officer's face.

John Williams took a notion one night and went into the woods, to live with the natives. This he had done in America, and been sorely whipped for it. He knew that natives starved like we did, but they did not flog each other. He was not seen for some weeks, then he came to the hut one night with a native man he called Daku. And like him, Williams was naked and filthy. They had a dog.

'How are you James?'

'Getting by. Counting the weeks now to my seven years. How are you living John?'

'By hunting, setting traps. Not easy.'

They had come to me for food, I was sure. I gave them pease and carrot and asked him if he knew whether the natives were planning to fight. He asked Daku, having learned some of their curious sounding words.

'He says you never asked about taking the fish and cutting away the land.'

I tried to imagine the governor with us, in my hut, asking Daku about the farm, but in my mind, the governor took one look at the man and walked away. After a month away, John Williams came back to his hut and began working on the farm again. Dodd was angry and had him put before the court. I asked Dodd if he would take me to the governor.

'Why?'

'Sir, I want to ask him about my time here. What with the hulk, it's nearly done.'

'Farmers can't go home Ruse, not until we have a farm,' he said. 'I have to make a report, you may come with me.'

I was brought to the governor's house; all the officers had houses. He was eating a pear, part of which he fed to a bat that he had tamed. It had fouled on the edge of his table on which there was a chart. At his feet were his two greyhounds. Dodd was full of praise and promise for the farm.

'The only problem is clearing the land, it wears men out. But the soil is as you would expect for any area close to shore.'

It was worse than Cornwall. As his servant spoke, the governor looked at me and he saw my thinking.

'Ruse. I remember you from the *Supply*. Mr Dodd here tells me you are most industrious on his farm.'

'I have to be sir, to get it to give anything.'

'Well the settlement is giving us the luxury of pears. But it is bread we need.'

'Sir, I wanted to ask, John Williams went into the woods with the natives. But he has helped us. The natives steal from the farm and attack the work party, but Williams he is acting as a go-between see.'

'He deserted us,' snapped Dodd, angry that I'd led him on. I went on, 'And if he is flogged again he will run away for good or else lay himself down. He is my best hand sir.'

'I shall speak to the court,' said the governor.

I didn't know what that meant. And I didn't know when I would be in the governor's house again. I chanced my arm.

'Sir, something else, I was on a hulk for four years.'

'Yes.'

'Well, with that time and the journey here last year, and this year now, I have served six years ....'

'I know what you're about to ask Ruse, and I must tell you I was given no records of how long any convict is to serve. The papers were meant to be on the transports but they were not.'

'Captain Tench, he knows.'

The governor got up and fed the bat a piece of a fig, like I'd seen growing on the fatal tree.

'My duty is to the survival of this settlement,' he said. 'I have a colony of villains, unfit subjects in a country that affords less assistance to new settlers than anywhere in the world. And you expect me to send men to England upon their word? Men I need.'

The bat's brown eyes shone, its mouth slapped on the fruit.

'I have sent to London for the papers, until then all convicts will remain here. You are going to make a new farm, up-river at Rose Hill. There, you will find the soil more agreeable than on Henry's farm.'

Peat and Bryant had it right. We were all there for the rest of our days. Our purpose was not to serve a sentence but to make a new country for others. The word was about and more convicts disappeared into the woods. Some tried to live with the natives but the natives did not want us. There was talk of an uprising, the court handing-out every greater floggings, one poor wretch, six hundred strokes for speaking ill of the governor.

It was, as far as I could tell, the turn of winter into spring, when we set out in two boats, up the river that runs into the harbour. The morning of the first day, we journeyed by sail, much after that it was all oars for two days against the current. There were nine of us convicts, Williams and Peat and McIntyre among them. The governor and Tench had brought a half-a-dozen marines and a servant of some sort. The water was the colour of the undergrowth that grew out of the river, hiding the banks from view. We came across many natives in canoes, mostly frightened of us, having seen us for the first time. Their boats were one long piece of bark tied at the ends. They paddled standing at the back, which took much balance, and they had mounds of soil in the centre of their little vessels, upon which they cooked the fish they had speared. The governor approached one canoe and gave the natives a shirt each.

'Look at him will yer,' said McIntyre. 'Thinks he's an emperor handing out bounty. Thinks more of the savages than he does us.'

We camped on a sand bar and though we had brought victuals Tench preferred to go on a hunting adventure.

'Never eat off the stores if you can live off the land.'

We were each given a handful of salt beef and a cup of water. The marines drank rum and the officers drank tea which they made from a leaf the surgeon claimed was fortifying. Tench came back with ducks, presenting them to the governor like a cat to its owner. We convicts sat apart under guard and were given no duck to eat; the smell of its fat on the pan was cruelty to us. A group of natives approached in two canoes. They were interested in our boat and one clambered in. A private went to throw him out but the governor said to leave him be. Then the governor gave the natives some of his men's duck to eat. Perhaps McIntyre was right. For him, the natives were like children, perfect in innocence and want. We were tainted souls, convicts lost to man and God, who would only be tamed by punishment. The court had sentenced Williams to a hundred lashes for desertion; the governor would not pardon him but reduced it to fifty. Williams asked me and Bryant not to be present. As the natives ate the duck, McIntyre looked on with murder in his eyes.

We were at the place the governor had called Rose Hill by noon the next day. It looked no different to any other landing along the river. Once we got beyond the watertrees, we were in grassland without any underwood or shrubs. The grass was bright, the colour of pondweed. A spring rain fell on us which the flowers were open to. I believed I was looking at a field known only to God.

CHAPTER 16

The Good Ground

By the middle of the following year we had cleared and we had planted seed once more for a November harvest. The soil looked middling to me, neither good nor bad. Our up-river farm was roughly the size of Cove Farm, but it had more promise, more convicts working on it and more hopes resting upon it. They called the new settlement Rose Hill, and left Captain Tench in charge of the camp and Dodd in charge of the farm. Tench I reckoned, was not happy with his posting and he was soon taking off into the back of beyond with two redcoats and a convict to carry his pots. There were a hundred or more of us at the start, and maybe some, tearing their arms by dragging out the trees, thought we were there to feed ourselves. I knew that the wheat, barley, and corn sown had to keep the cove alive as well. If we failed, we would starve, by the hundred. Some would starve even if the harvest was good, for it was six months away.

The *Sirius* came back from The Cape, but the half rations we were on never got more. They had planted on Norfolk Island but still took from the stores. The river could not feed us like the sea, though we plundered it for the eels, one of which was near a day's ration. Redcoats would walk into the wilderness for game and not return, which pleased me. Two went looking for the leaves we made sweet tea from and were never seen again. A month later, others came back with a large rat and a jacket, saying they had found the men burned on a fire and their clothes hung up in a tree in triumph. We'd see natives in dead men's shirts and Tench warned against leaving the farm, for all the woodland looked the same to us, so few the trees in variety, and no mountain, no spire to position against, just the quiet river that wandered and hid.

One day, an emu came tiptoeing into the camp to excitement on its part and ours. It was shot and plucked and when cut open was found to have dozens of eggs inside, more than twice the size of a duck's. No convict was given its meat or eggs, for all of that went to our masters. We were the last for everything, no matter what fine words the governor had said at the cove. Williams was right when he spoke of being a slave, we all were, not owned by some squire but by the King of England, with Tench and the governor as overseers. We had made a farm at the cove, good for nothing but more seed and blood, and now we had to do it all again. We were back to living in tents and building huts for our masters, first for Tench and his officers, then for the rest, lastly our own. The work killed. A man digging a trench staggered away to a spot in the shade and lay down, declaring, 'Put me here, will you?'

When we put him in the ground that same evening, someone said the richer soil would make digging graves easier. Bryant's words about England's reckoning came back to me, for since I had been seized in South Petherwin some seven years before, I had prayed most days, for forgiveness, for mercy, for Susanna and Richard, for the harvest. Now I prayed for vengeance, for every redcoat and officer was as idle as any squire at home; many as much a crook as Thomas Olive. I blamed my starvation and my pains on the loss of commons and the price of grain and rent, and my anger kept me alive. My heart burned to live by my own hand and not have others live from it. I was Dodd's overseer once more, but in England and New Holland too I lived in the prison of the landless.

Soon after our camp by the river had a name and a sawpit, it had a gallows tree. A man, maybe in the midst of life but seeming to have lived more than one, was brought straight from the officers' tent to the trunk of it. Redcoats herded us to watch. There was no lesson from the Bible, no reverend of solace, just a corporal's plain call.

'This man stole someone's clothes.'

And then the wretch's final words, 'I can't say why I took them. I couldn't help myself, that's all.'

He suffered a long, twisting choke. His name I never knew. In the tent at night, Charles Peat was weeping.

'I don't understand a hanging for taking a smock and trousers,' he said. 'It's not the same as food. The food's eaten, it's gone. A man needs food to live, but the clothes they can be given back to him.'

'He would have only stolen them again,' said Williams.

'Are you saying he deserved to be turned-off, for taking some garments from a tent?' I asked.

'He couldn't stop stealing, is all I'm saying,' said Williams.

Charles Peat hid his face with his hands.

'Are you all right, Mr Peat?' I asked.

He took his hands away and looked at nothing.

'I was thinking of Barrett. He cut a key you know, for the food store.'

'He was clever, was Barrett,' said Williams.

'He was. Other people might have kicked in the door. But I am partly to blame,' said Peat. 'I told a redcoat that he was a coiner, and could cut a key for him. I think the redcoat made him and then he peached on him.'

'They give you something for that whisper?' asked Williams.

'He gave me a piece of pork.'

The natives up-river hadn't seen us before and more than at the cove they didn't want us there. At first, they treated us much the same. They smiled, took gifts, stole hatchets, took us to a stream. As we cut down more trees, marked-out more land, their character towards us altered. There was one among them who the others looked-up to, and he walked across our farm with two or three others behind him, making threats to one of us after another. He was bigger than the others, with a bone through his nose, an in-turned eye, and foot. He once said something in McIntyre's direction, who squared up to him.

'I don't like the way you're looking at me, you stub-faced half cripple. You want to go into the woods and sort this do you? Be my guest.'

The native understood well and replied in his own tongue, saying what I judged as, 'I am not frightened of you, I am not a guest, and neither are you. I will come back and kill you and others.'

The natives killed our livestock. What redcoats there were, for there were mercifully few at Rose Hill, were put on sentry day and night. Then, like a storm coming upon the harbour, a pox arrived and natives began to die all around us. *A pestilence that walketh in darkness, a destruction that wasteth at noonday* fed and thrived upon them. The pox pushed-up their skin like toadstools on dying trees, bodies bubbling white; much more on the children and the old. There were so many, they could not bury their own, but left corpses on the riverbank, and all about in the woods. Some of the afflicted walked into our camp, once, two women and a boy, wide-eyed and limp. I was with Williams and the others, plucking caterpillars from the corn. We did not go to them, but kept our distance. Some convicts threw stones at them, tried to chase them back to the woods, but the family were desolate, utterly at our mercy. Mr Dodd and the surgeon brought them into their hut. The two women were dead the next day, but the boy was nursed to health, given the name Billy and lived on with Mr Dodd and the Surgeon. Billy was clothed and content in our camp, Williams giving him chores. I'd put him at ten-years-old.

By the time of the harvest, there were few natives to be seen. Though convicts had been pillaging from the crop, it was a bountiful harvest, with two hundred and more bushels of wheat and thirty or more of barley. The wheat heads drooped with long spikes and gold coated seeds. Indian corn shone in the New Holland sun. The governor came up to Rose Hill to see this splendid thing in a barge named the *Rose Hill Packet*, but which we convicts called the *Lump*, for it looked like a carriage on water. It was built to take food and all else back and forward and was the slowest article afloat. The governor stood with me and Dodd and smiled, or perhaps it was the sun in his eyes.

'You will need a bigger barn up here. I must see if I can get you a ship's carpenter,' said the governor. 'The barn at the cove is barely needed. A handful of bushels from twenty acres. Henceforth this shall be the colony's farm. Get it cut and on the boat as soon as you can.'

They went into Dodd's hut for some wine, I was told to wait outside. I looked at the fields and weighed-up that I had rarely seen a harvest to match it in Cornwall, and this virgin soil, without much manure, tended mainly by the half-starved, ignorant idle, assailed by rats and all else that crawled. It was moist, riverbank soil and dry heat. The day before, I had seen Dodd dig up a cabbage near twenty pound in weight. Tench called me in to the hut. They were seated, but I stood.

'Ruse, we were just discussing,' said Tench, 'how long it would be for a man to become self-sufficient here, that is off the stores and feeding himself. And how many acres he would require to achieve that. We wondered what your opinion was.'

'Well, sir. I'd say you'd need two acres maybe, and a year. And you'd need some livestock to get by.'

'And you'd need to be industrious,' said Dodd wagging a finger.

The governor coughed, and there was silence.

'I looked into your term Ruse, and Tench confirms that your time has expired. So, as of this moment you are a free man. But I want you to think on something. You could get the *Packet* to the cove and there wait for a ship to work your passage home, but I can tell you none is expected. Or, I am prepared to give you two acres of your own to work, until you can come off the stores. You can have some livestock, a hut of your own, labourers. And if you can prove self-sufficient in that year you talk about, I will grant the land to you as your own property.'

Dodd and Tench smiled in approval, the governor handed me a chit saying I was *emancipated.* I was expected to jump for joy. My seven years had been up in July, it was now November. For my freedom, I was being offered another year's hard labour, but then I would own the land. More than likely, once I stepped out of Dodd's hut, I would not be in Cornwall in a year anyway.

'My land?' I asked.

The governor nodded slowly.

'You will be the first settler here. You were the first ashore, were you not, in Botany Bay? Lieutenant Johnston on your back.'

At which Tench and Dodd laughed. He went on, 'Seems only right you should be the first convict to have some land.'

I looked at my chit again. I had been flattered, I felt proud of something, but I didn't know what.

'Are we agreed?' he asked.

'We are,' I said.

I went to the hut I shared with Williams, Peat, and McIntyre. Williams was sitting on the ground outside as usual, for he did not like the darkness of it.

'The governor has spoken to me,' I said. 'My seven years up, he has made me a free man.'

I showed them the chit. No-one said anything at first. Charles Peat shook my hand.

'Are you going back?' asked Williams.

'Not yet,' I said.

'Can you *get* back? asked McIntyre.

'You have to work your passage home,' I said.

'Are there ships leaving? There wasn't a mast in the harbour when we left there,' he said.

I shook my head.

'I've been given a couple of acres to work. If I can grow, he says I can keep it.'

'A settler?' asked McIntyre. 'In this poxy place?'

'I'll be the first.'

'You mean, apart from the king,' replied McIntyre.

'Will you have your own slaves?' asked John Williams.

'No, I will not,' I said.

But the next day, half-starved, weary men were put to clearing two acres for me and building me a hut. I asked Williams to work on the hut, for I had shown him how to cut grooves in the wood, so it would hold together. There were few nails to be had anywhere. The same night, natives tore it down, set fire to the wheat crop, and speared a redcoat. A party was sent into the woods to bring back the head of their leader, the man with the in-turned eye and foot, for there had been reports of his attacks at the cove as well. It had been nearly two years since we had arrived on the land, and the pox had taken so many, but it seemed the natives were at last gathering an army to fight with. Their leader, this man with the limp, was called Pemulwuy. I wondered whether there would be killing for me to have land, whether I would have to kill for it.

I was given new clothes from the stores on account of being a free man. To mark it myself, I took the *Lump* to the cove to see Will and Mary.

I sailed back with the governor and sat upon the deck nearby him, but always, free as I was, I found it hard to look him in the eye man to man. As we got closer to the harbour, convicts were labouring on the riverbank.

'I'm having a road built all the way to Rose Hill. Soon there will be carts carrying grain to Sydney Cove. And a road to Botany Bay as well, along the track the natives use.'

It was a year since I'd left the cove. There was now a wide street of stone, barracks made of brick. Men were constructing a wharf; a horse dragged the trunk of a tree. I saw the fishing cutter, far out into the water. I wondered who was aboard, for after his flogging for keeping back fish, Will had been taken off the boat and put on the farm. I sat on the rocks and looked at the work of the settlement. The woods all around had been cleared and there were now great squares of land marked out. Natives still fished from their bark canoes, but there were fewer than a year before. The marines stood at their posts, they wore ragged coats bleached pink by the salty air and sun. One strode over to me, 'You, why aren't you working?'

I took the chit out of my pocket, held it aloft.

'I'm a free man now. Given this, by the governor himself.'

'Stand-up, when you speak to me.'

I stood while he looked at the paper, confused I thought.

'That word, says *emancipated*,' I said, helpfully.

He looked at me oddly, as I'd seen people look the first time they had seen a kangaroo, an animal that didn't make sense to them. He sniffed and gave me my chit back.

'Best move along. Go do something useful with your freedom.'

I walked the mile to Farm Cove and saw Mary scratching at the parched earth with a hoe, Charlotte waddling behind her. Charlotte had a roughly cut white smock on, and a hat made of rushes. I bent down and looked into her little blue eyes. Born on the voyage she was like me I thought, a first, first child of the colony. I picked her up.

'You're the first New Holland girl.'

'I hope to take her home someday,' said Mary, 'make her Cornish. How are you James Ruse?'

'I've been made a free man.'

I showed her my paper, she was happy for me.

'How much longer have you to do?'

'Two years,' said Mary.'

She told me that Will was back on the boat, with James Martin who I knew from the hulk, and was living in my old hut. Then she said, 'I am with child again James.'

I was surprised she had told me this without Will there since it was his first child, but she seemed frightened of something.

Will and James Martin arrived and we embraced.

'Back on the boat Will Bryant,' I said.

'Aye and James with me. They sent you back here?'

'James is a free man now,' said Mary.

I nodded. 'Your time will be up as well Will.'

'Won't make no difference to me. For Mary's isn't. Not for another two years. And she's expecting again. And I hear the only way back is to work your passage. Can't work my passage with a family. What will you do James?'

'I don't know. I have the promise of land if I can make a couple of acres work.'

'What you've always wanted.'

'What I always wanted in Cornwall,' I replied.

The huts were much improved since last year. Shingle roofs and wooden floors. It was James Martin's work.

'They started making the barracks out of brick, so I asked for their wood. Shingle keeps the water out. Seems it never rains here but once a month, to wash everything away.'

'Way I see it,' said Will Bryant, 'out here, you'll never be free. Redcoats on your back, natives to fight, starvation rations. You say you're free. Is there a tavern to go to for free men? You're just going to have to work this Godforsaken land, like you have the last two years.'

'James says the land up-river is good,' said Mary.

But Will shook his head, for he had a different type of hunger to me.

I stayed with them for a few days, if only because I had the leisure to do so. Then I went back to Rose Hill. My hut was finished but already with rats for we were plagued by them. I made a pen for my livestock and helped clear the rest of the two acres. My hut and my land was set apart from Rose Hill Farm, a little walk away, on a track through a clump of gum trees. At the end of a day I'd often go to the convict hut with Williams, Peat and the others, for I was lonely, and McIntyre would fleer at me saying, 'Well Ruse, tell us how things are for the man that is free? Must be wonderful to be so free, mustn't it?'

Convicts had been told to keep away from my land and my hut and if they stole from my garden I could have them flogged. Williams and Peat were as sociable as they were before, but many were not, some thought me a spy. There would have been company for me had there been others who had been granted freedom, but at that time there wasn't. In the end the coldness of others and a word from Mr Dodd with a hatchet made me sleep in the hut they had built for me. Really, it was Dodd that was in charge of Rose Hill for Tench was away weeks at a time, exploring. Unlike the officers, Dodd worked in the field, worked harder than anyone. For that he had respect, as much respect as convicts would give any master. He did not stand around giving orders all day, and he could get men to work without the threat of a flogging.

Natives would come and camp a few days at a time, fish in the river nearby. They'd ask for food by pointing to their mouths but we hadn't much to give them save some turnips, for the good harvest hadn't changed much in the way of rations. Some would come alone, a woman, a child; their families most likely taken by the pox. They were not always taken in by others, so stayed at the camp with us. There was one that Williams gave much attention to; a bonny woman he took to. He gave her food from his kitchen garden, fished for her after labour and sat with her, listening to her strange sounding words. We would not see her for days and then she would return, standing at the edge of the woods, until she saw Williams. Apart from her we were at that time a camp of no women, and she was right to be afeared of us. She came one night to shelter from lashing rain, so I took her into my hut rather than a hut of ten men. 'James, James's hut' I said to her a few times. And she came back saying the same. After I told Williams this, he brought her to my hut one night, holding her by the hand. I walked out leaving them alone, standing in the warm rain, the gathering puddles. Her name was Binda and she would sing songs that were pleasing. She walked lightly on her feet as if the earth was covered with ice. Soon Williams was following her about when he should have been working, sitting by a fire with her, she uttering English words and he her words. When the reverend came up to Rose Hill that Christmas Day, Binda stood in the congregation with the surgeon's adopted boy and other natives. What they believed I never knew, but thought them as close to God as any that stood in a church. Williams, he asked the reverend if he would marry him to Binda, so they could have their own hut. His request was denied and I thought he would go into the woods once more, but they stayed as they were, him sleeping in his men's hut, she on the ground outside it.

When I lived in the cove, we would look each day for the sight of a mast, a ship from somewhere bringing us food, but it never came. In the middle of the third year of New Holland, that year being 1790, a ship did come to the cove, bringing only more convicts, women convicts. They were to us men most welcome but I wondered how they would be fed. It also brought to my mind what Peat had said to me on the *Scarborough*, 'We are livestock James.' Many of the women from the convict ship were sent to Rose Hill, for we were a place without any. Every week the *Lump* brought a score or so to work the farm. I had Williams working for me and thought I would ask for a woman too, because I wanted a woman for myself. I went and looked at them, watched them work. They were thin, in a poorer state than ourselves; ragged and barefoot, as if they had come from some other plantation where they had laboured for years. Many were not walking well and though it was winter there, and cooler, the heat was too much a burden for them. Few could move more than a handful of earth with each stroke. It wasn't long before one fell to her knees and then keeled. Some others ran to her.

'Bring her here,' cried Dodd.

Three women carried her over and Dodd and me lifted her to some shade. The fainted woman was the oldest on the field, her hair white and lank, flesh on her face gone grey too. There was lice on her, lice on the other three. They wafted her with palm leaves, the youngest helped herself to the water barrel and trickled water on the old woman's face, saying, 'Come on Martha, wake-up, time to wake-up, Martha.'

And when Martha came around dry-retching, the younger woman laughed and hugged her saying, 'Must have been the sight of all these fine men, made you faint.'

Then she looked up at Dodd and said, 'I ought to sit here with her a while, don't you think sir?'

Before Dodd could answer, I butted in, 'I think you should. I'll make some tea for you.'

I brought two cups between the four and sat next to her.

'You look like you all need a saints' day off,' I said.

'Reckon I look like I need to be fed and washed,' she said. 'How come they don't have you working?'

'I do work. On my own land.'

'They should have transported me to your land. Where is your land?'

'Well, not my land yet, but it will be. I served my time see.'

'And you'd rather have some land in hell than go home, would you?'

I didn't know what to say at first, for it was true.

'I will go home, few years from now. But I've been given a chance to have my own farm, and I've always wanted my own land. I ended-up here, for stealing silver to buy a place on a farm. Wouldn't you like somewhere to sit, that you owned yourself?'

Other women had started to walk off the field and sit down and Dodd was calling them all back to work. I watched her for a while, fixing her shape, her face into my mind. Next day I went to Dodd and asked if I could have her for my two acres.

'The governor said I could have convicts to help me if I needed.'

'And you need her do you? A half-starved slip of a girl. I doubt if she'll bring in the bushels, but you can have her if you want her.'

'I do.'

I went straight up to her and said, 'Come with me.'

'Why?'

'You're to work with me.'

'Just me?'

She looked around at the other women; some had stopped work and were looking at me, fearful for her I think.

'I just need a little bit of help that's all, if you wouldn't mind. Just on the next fields.'

'Where?'

'That way.'

She looked to the older woman Martha, like she was her mother, so I said, 'I have a good kitchen garden, you'd have something to bring back.'

Martha shrugged and nodded.

I remember watching her walk towards me, walking beside me carrying a hoe, young and womanly, even in rags.

'Were you brought up on a farm?' I asked.

'Dairy farm. Not scratching the ground like a peasant.'

'But you know, working on a farm, it ain't like working anywhere else.'

'Course I know. Which is why I ran away and ended-up thieving,' she said.

'Me, I was bred a husbandman.'

'But you ended-up thieving 'n all.'

'So that I might be a proper farmer. This is my place here. Up to the woods.'

She looked at the land, where I had pulled a wooden plough strapped to my back, like it was a midden. Looked at the chickens, the hogs, my ramshackle hut, downcast she was. I thought about telling her I'd choose someone else if she didn't like it but I fancied her hair cut like a boy's, the same colour as her eyes, and her small mouth. She was lean from under-feeding but there was still a roundness and a fullness and I wanted her.

'You own this, do you?'

'The governor's saying I can, if I can grow crops. Then I reckon I'll be able to sell the crops to him.'

'What's in the ground?'

'Wheat. I sowed in May. Putting in maize soon.'

'You could do with a couple of cows.'

'I know that,' I said.

'What do you want me to do?' she asked.

'I have a couple of pits over there. We need to fill them with straw, anything we can't dig in, until it rots down. I make me own manure see.'

Williams, who was down the other end, burning roots, walked up to us asking, 'Is she working with us?'

'She is,' I said.

He said nothing, only staring at her for too long.

'My name is Elizabeth,' she said.

He said nothing but carried on staring. She got to it with her hands and a rake. I sent Williams back to his fire and worked near her, digging in weeds. The ashes from Williams' fire would be dug in the next day. Anything that would feed the soil, I used. Then Williams found his tongue and came back and forth to talk to her. *Where are you from? Are you here for life, like me? I was in Virginia seven years.* The next day I had him work with Dodd so I could be alone with her. I made her tea for she liked it, and roasted some carrots. She was stamping straw down in the pit when she screamed and jumped out of it, her leg folding under her. I had made a pit for a snake, long and brown like a quartermaster's belt. There were two holes in her calf put by needles, no bleeding. She sat up.

'Don't move,' I said.

'Only a bite,' she said.

'It has poison. You have poison in you, if you move about it will only move about inside you. The natives told us you have to sit and wait.'

'How long?'

'A week, maybe.'

She cursed me and my farm and the home I had made for a snake. I got the surgeon, Surgeon Harris. He bandaged all the way up her leg above the bite, he said to stop the flow of poison. Then we carried her to the women's hut where she lay for five days. Snakes had taken some men away; most had survived after days of flux and fever, the limb swelling-up like risen dough. I went back to the pit and hacked up the snake then went looking for others to kill.

I got permission to go into the hut when the other women were working. I brought her tea, a pea broth, onions, fruit I begged off Dodd, anything I could. I asked Binda to make a medicine from plants she knew, and Williams to catch eels. I got her a new smock dress from the stores and burned her old clothes. Elizabeth didn't have much pain with the bite but there were days when she had no feeling on one side of her body, and she cried with the fear that I had made her a cripple. I stroked her head, we told each other our histories. She had been sent away for seven years for stealing garments. One morning I was on my way to her and she limped out of the hut into the light. I held out my hand, she took it.

'I've been told I have to go back to work.'

She walked warily to Dodd's farm, Martha coming to greet her with a steady arm. I had Williams brought back to work for me, and he never said a word about me sending him away. I got it into my mind that I would just have to choose another woman. I was then gone thirty years-of-age, without children beyond Richard, who I doubted I would ever set eyes on again. I finished preparing my ground for maize; I thought few women would turn down a free man with land. I was pulling my plough behind me the earth holding me to a standstill, when a redcoat brought Elizabeth through the gum trees that divided my farm from Dodd's.

'This one's back with you now Ruse.'

Elizabeth stood with her hands on her hips.

'How are you?' I asked her.

'The others said I had to work for you, and bring back what vegetables I could.'

'And that's why you're here is it?'

She was never going to say otherwise. It was always the way of the settlement. Women used their scarcity to give themselves the upper hand.

'I need to get you some shoes, don't I?'

I put her to broadcasting behind my plough, in the hope she'd want to see something grow. Something seemed to have changed in her since the snakebite. She had accepted where she was and that she would be staying, and she would try to make the best of it. A lot of convicts never did that. The next day she went into the hut and complained that it was too small, but didn't say for what. In the months between then and the harvest she would hardly let me touch her, and I tried many times. Then as the maize we had planted together began to grow strong, we lay together in my hut. I spent evenings making the hut bigger and making the bed bigger. This took until nearly harvest when Captain Tench came to see how 'the experiment' as he liked to call it was working. I showed him about and said I had no longer any need of the stores. I told him I had done all this without the aid of manure, and showed him my pits where I rotted everything down. He wrote it all in his notebook which he liked to do. He said I should go to the cove with the grain and see the governor about his promise.

The road to Rose Hill was half-way made, there was another year of brick buildings at the cove, more convicts than ever, dragging stone, timber, carts of bricks, a flogging underway. A stone road led up the hill to the governor's house which was brick made and whitewashed. There were two sentries in the garden outside.

'State your business.'

'I'm here to see the governor. I've brought grain from Rose Hill.'

I was nodded through the door. Then there was another man outside another door, 'Name?'

'James Ruse.'

He knocked and waited and went in. Then he came out and told me to go in. The governor was looking at a map.

'Captain Tench tells me in a letter the experiment has worked. You're off the stores.'

'I am sir.'

'That's good. If you can do it, then so can others.'

'Just needs hard work sir.'

He looked away from the map, right at me.

'That's not easy to come by. Another four convict transports have just arrived. Half of them too sick to work, the other half too idle. This country needs men like you to settle here. Forget England Ruse, I'm giving you another thirty acres. A land grant. The first.'

He passed me a sheet of paper and his pen.

'You need to sign it.'

I didn't do so because I wasn't sure I'd heard him correctly. I looked at the paper and found the word I was looking for, 'thirty.'

'Sign it at the bottom,' he said.

Then he came round the table and shook my hand. I remember thinking, this is a man, who might have met the king, or who knew men that had, and he is shaking my hand.

'Sir, I wondered if you knew if William Bryant was still the fisherman, for the cove?'

Then the small hint of a smile fled from his face.

'Why do you ask about him?'

'I was on a hulk with him, four years. I'd like to give him the news while I'm here, about my grant, see his child.'

He walked back round his desk.

'Bryant has gone. Escaped with his family, seven others. Been gone a week, and in my cutter. Well planned we think. We had nothing in the harbour to chase them in.'

CHAPTER 17

The Flight

Evans was over two weeks late. That is if he was ever coming at all, for we all silently believed the storm had taken the *Speedwell*. We had stopped killing seals. We'd worked our way round the whole island leaving blood and gore in every bay, on every rocky bluff. We were back where Evans had asked us to be, waiting. And so were the seals, floundering over the sand, mocking us, for all the slaughter had been for nothing. Our sealskins would never be sold in London, because they would never leave the island, and neither would we.

Williams was no less gloomy than he ever was. Scottish Jack had taken to meandering along the edge of the sea, picking up driftwood.

'See this piece of timber, it's from the *Speedwell*. Look at it. That's our ship.'

McIntyre spat, sucked on his pipe, looked past Jack.

'This goose thinks our lives are in the hands of some spirits.'

'We should never have come here,' said Jack.

'*You* should never have come,' said McIntyre. 'The rest of us have been in scrapes before.'

I tried to brighten the mood, thought it my duty.

'There is an obvious reason why Evans isn't here, that we haven't talked about.'

'Do enlighten us James,' said McIntyre.

'He's either not got enough skins, or he's got plenty but he wants more, because there are more seals, and greed has got a hold of him.'

'Right, let me get this straight,' said McIntyre. 'What you're telling us is our boat hasn't come for us because the sealing out there is either good, or it's because it's not good. That's your theory James Ruse, is it?'

'The storm took him,' said Scottish Jack.

'I wouldn't be so sure,' said McIntyre. 'He could have found some shelter for her. Evans is a fool, but he's not mad. He's greedy enough to take risks but not so greedy that he'd risk his own life. He's not here because Evans is Evans is all, he always treats his crews like shit.'

'There!'

Scottish Jack flung out his right arm.

'See it?'

We could see a square mast, face on, low in the water, then another.

'What's he doing away to the north?' asked McIntyre.

'Maybe he was blown off course,' said Williams.

'That's not the *Speedwell*,' I said. 'And it's not coming here.'

The sails turned east and showed us a third mast.

'She'll be a whaler, heading for the mainland,' said McIntyre.

The mainland was a blemish to the north, the smaller island to the west clearer.

'The whaling season is almost done. We could be here another year, before someone even passes,' said Scottish Jack.

No-one replied for we were all downcast. Williams got to his feet and walked to the sea. I thought for a moment he was about to walk into it. He looked-out for a few minutes then walked back to us.

'How long do we give Evans?' asked Williams.

'Before what?' asked McIntyre.

'Before leaving.'

McIntyre laughed.

'Where are we going?'

Williams pointed north.

'The mainland.'

'In what?' asked Scottish Jack.

'The boat.'

'It's got a hole in it the size of a cannonball. So many cracks all over the place. It can't be repaired,' said McIntyre.

'It can. We can cover it with skins. Stitch them together.'

'Stitch them with what?' I asked.

'The guts of birds, fish, the seals. Make a needle with bone. Boil bones, the paste will keep the water out. And we can make a frame for a hood.'

Williams' notion met with silence. No heads nodded and none shook either. We all hesitated to ask more, to be hopeful.

'You've done this before have you Williams?' asked McIntyre, almost politely.

'I saw natives do it in Virginia?'

'Why the mainland?' I asked.

'There'll be no more shelter on the next island. Even if Evans is alive, I'd say his boat's wrecked or sunk. Mainland's twenty miles or so away. Between us, we could row there. Day-and-a-half.'

'Could be that Evans is doing repairs on the *Speedwell*, that's why he's late,' ventured Scottish Jack.

'Oh aye, there'll be a boatyard on a deserted island,' said McIntyre.

'We could prepare a large fire, for the next whaler. It might pick us up,' I said.

'Whalers make Evans look like the Good Samaritan,' said McIntyre.

Williams started carelessly throwing pebbles at the surf. He was rarely taken seriously by other men, but he was sure of his plan, and it was all we had.

'That strait John, it's squallish and treacherous fast,' I warned.

'We don't fight it. We just cut away from it, a piece at a time. And if we stay here another month,' he said, 'we'll all die of the scurvy anyway.'

He was right. Before the bleeding comes the fatigue, and the melancholy. We would most likely starve before the sickness took us all.

Williams and Scottish Jack worked on covering the hull in skins; me and McIntyre on a frame for the hood. We went back to the trees, cut down some saplings we could weave, fastened them together with bark. A gap was left in the hood for the oarsmen, there were two layers of skins. It was the first time that all four of us had combined and the labour lifted our spirits. When we first put it in the water we cheered aloud. It is a craft indeed.

'Those Indians who made these,' McIntyre asked Williams, 'how far did they go in them?'

'Long ways.'

'And what was the sea like, like this was it?'

'It wasn't the sea, they just sailed them in the river.'

'A river, a flaming river? God help us all.'

The morning of our departure was clearer than any of our time on the island; I believed I could make out features on the land in the distance. Williams had the craft in the water, tightening the hood; McIntyre was bundling-up as many of our skins as we could take, and Scottish Jack was filling the water barrel. All of a sudden, Williams stopped work and looked down the beach. He didn't point but held on to his stare. I questioned him but he didn't answer. I went down to the boat, waded into the surf to look along his view and saw a canoe beyond the rocks. The craft had a tail, pointing-up like a turkey's. We were about to walk over when, from out of the dunes, two natives came running, crying-out harshly, wielding wooden sticks. McIntyre and Scottish Jack readied themselves, McIntyre with the rifle, Scottish Jack with his knife. Williams and me, we dragged in the boat and joined the fray. Between the four of us we stabbed and clubbed them many times, Scottish Jack cutting their throats like they were goats. Then we looked about us to see if there were more, which there were, four more on the grass above, circling us.

'To the boat,' I shouted.

Me and Williams, we stepped backwards to the water, Williams brandished an oar.

'Jack,' I shouted, 'this way.'

But he bid the natives on, crouching and swaying, digging his heels into the sand. As we pushed the boat into the water they came for him, killed him with their clubs. McIntyre ran for the boat, and as he reached for it Williams raised his oar and struck it down on his skull. McIntyre went under the reddening water. Williams began rowing for his life, and so did I.

CHAPTER 18

What is Thy Country?

Rose Hill, New Holland, 1791

The reverend married us on a spring morning, four other couples with us. People clapped and threw flowers for we were not without our joys. We showed the reverend our house, brick built, the wood from the hut put to the floor. We gave him raspberries, lilly pillies and tea.

'I have a vineyard now,' he said. 'Cucumbers like you've never seen.'

'How are your children, reverend?' asked Elizabeth.

'They thrive. We have given our latest a native name, Milbah, and the native girl we adopted helps about the house and garden. If only I had a church.'

'Surely there are enough convicts to build you one,' I said.

'The conditions on the second fleet were disgraceful. Many are still too weak to work, some will never recover. There are so few carpenters here. So, I minister outside, or when it rains, in the boathouse.'

'My father used to say, *a house cannot make the carpenter*,' I said.

'He was a Methodist?'

'A lay preacher, and I reckon he still is.'

The reverend's lesson that morning had been about the house of man and the house of God, as always trying to comfort his congregation in their want. *If the tent that is our earthly home is destroyed, we have a building from God, a house not made with hands.* But I knew it was his own spirits he was lifting also, since after three years in New Holland, no-one would build him a church. It was a Sunday, free from labour and John Williams came over with Binda. Binda had made some wattle seed bread, more biscuit than bread but not unpleasing. She was clothed and could speak some broken English. In company, she would often speak more than Williams. He and her swapped tongues but could read each other in silence. Elizabeth and me, we wore our voices out quarrelling, but never hesitated with the marriage. She never liked John Williams, but could not see through Peat and McIntyre, wanted me to call her Betty not Elizabeth, kept asking me why my farm wasn't closer to the river, and talked too much about her adventures in London. For me, it was the loneliness of the seven years before that I took spite with. Elizabeth though, she needed foes in her life.

'Binda is spying for the natives, and she'll be with them not us when they come.'

She said she would never turn her back on Williams.

'He has the face of a cut-throat. Eyes made of painted glass.'

On Sundays, we would walk the mile or so up to the river and we would sit or we would bathe in the mossy water. There were three other men given their freedom and thirty acres after me, but they had not an acre cleared when they started, and no house built for them. That first year of the farm, I had just eleven acres cleared, but any more cleared would have only meant more thieving by creatures, convicts and natives. They took any fruit half-ripe, any vegetable half-grown, any corn or wheat they could chew. Some nights I'd walk my land with a stave swinging it at a gang of them. Mr Dodd struggled even more, for there was fifty acres to chase men round and he couldn't count on his overseers. Rain never kept them off either and he spent so many nights sodden as a scarecrow he took to a fever and died. We had a service for his passing, and the governor praised the man who had been his servant for twenty years, saying what a fine gardener he was, mentioning the pumpkin-sized cabbage he had grown. The reverend recited *The Lord is My Shepherd*, those that could recited alongside him, but there were some bowed heads in the gathering who had good reason to look down.

Then one Sunday we came back to our house to find the door broken off and my other clothes all taken.

'If we don't stop this, I may as well go back and live in the women's hut, you in the men's hut, for we can't have a home when people come in and take what little we have.'

I went to stop it, went from hut to hut with my stave, muscling my way in, until I found a man standing in my trousers, like he was trying them on in a tailor's. He was an old man, my trousers sagging off him. I put the end of my stave under his chin.

'Name?' I said quietly.

He just shook his head. In the corner on the ground I could see my pillowcase. He hadn't a bed, just a blanket, not able to make one for himself. I lifted my stave such that his heels came up.

'Did you burgle my house for these?'

He began a babble talk, looking one way then another, pointing at nothing.

'McDonagh!' he cried out.

'Where? Where is he!' I demanded, prodding his chest with my stave.

I dragged him out of his hut like I was pulling a sheep out of a pen for butchery.

'Show me!'

He turned about full circle like a drunk out of a tavern, pointed to a row of huts by a half-made road. He nodded at one hut. I went in, found McDonagh's woman wearing my smock, him in my other trousers.

'Take it off,' I yelled at her.

Then I swung my stave at McDonagh putting him into the wall, went to his woman, and pulled my smock off her. McDonagh shouted after me, 'If you peach Ruse...'

Once I would have had my clothes back, gone home for a cup of rum. But my station in the world had improved. I had property and a wife. My property was not my clothes, it was my land, and I was surrounded by men who had nothing, and who only knew how to take. I took the old man to the barracks, dropped my stave on the way, and made him explain to a sergeant.

'McDonagh gave them to me because mine were threads, I had no pillowcase, but I did not go into this man's hut, on my life.'

'It will be your life,' said the sergeant.

I had my trousers off him and he was given some from the stores if he would agree to say the same in front of the magistrates. I told myself it was him, the old man that had peached, and not I, but when it came to standing before the three magistrates it was different. I had to condemn McDonagh to their faces and to his. I did it because people were still coming to our farm, filching food from the ground. When McDonagh was sentenced to two hundred lashes and to wear an iron collar for six months I went cold.

'What did the magistrates give him?' asked Elizabeth.

'Hundred lashes,' I lied.

She was wringing-out my smock over a tub.

'Will he be able to bear it?'

'He will live, by the looks of him. But he will not be able to bear it, no,' I said.

'It will make him think again.'

'I shouldn't have gone to the redcoats, I shouldn't. I saw a man hanged here, before you came, for stealing some clothes. I still see it in my mind. It was only trousers.'

'I have to be safe in this house James.'

'Didn't they send you here for stealing clothes, wasn't that what you done?'

She pegged it on the line between the branches, pulled out the creases, took a breath.

'I am with child, James,' she said.

'When is it coming?'

'Martha says August.'

This news, that I knew would come, had sealed my future I thought. For it would be harder to return to England with a child, even after Elizabeth's sentence had been served. Though Will Bryant and Mary, they had made their escape with two children, one only an infant, such was their hatred of captivity. Stories went about of their escape. The tools that they had secured, the cleverness and the quietness of its planning, by the tides and the moon. It was said that the captain of a Dutch ship had given them navigation instruments. I wondered where on the earth they were that night.

McDonagh was flogged right after being sentenced. I didn't watch but I saw him with his iron collar on, stumbling in half-steps on Dodd's farm, leg's apart to stay upright, hands holding the iron so it didn't break the skin. I knew from experience he would be carrying the weight of the lashes after the collar was gone.

The road to the cove was finished and a bridge across the river made. A chain of ponds was dug to keep eels and other fish. We were quarrying another town out of the ground and the soil was kinder at Rose Hill, but all else fought us. We could take the land from the trees and shrubs and make it our own, but the creatures did not leave with the undergrowth. The more convicts were sent to us, the more rats found their way to us. They would herd themselves, and from a distance looked like one great writhing creature scuttling over the ground. They could climb the walls of the house, at night we would hear their feet and their teeth on the roof above us. There were so many in the evenings we could club them as easy as seals. There were caterpillars to contend with, so abundant we could only wait for the rains to rid us of them. One day in July, a group of bats the size of kittens, with the look of fox cubs, came to roost. That night they left, but the next day, more than twice the number were in the trees, and more the day after. A bat in Cornwall you could fit into the palm of your hand, its wings spread. These, their wings out, were from forefinger to elbow. At sundown they chirruped like starlings; in the air they looked like hawks. People were afeared of them, of the multitude. I wondered at their presence; for they did not eat anything we had or grew. At night they seemed to feed in the skies, by day they hung asleep on high, like a warning of something to come.

The rains that had come before in the winter months never came that year. The heat, the dryness and stillness never ended when the days short-ened. The vermin multiplied; there was no relief from the insects, from the sores they gave us. Hotness can sap hunger, but Elizabeth needed nourishment and we had long ago eaten our livestock. Eleven acres of cleared land was no use to me in a drought, so I went to the officers' quarters to see Tench.

'I have to see Captain Tench.'

The sergeant didn't raise his face from the map he was studying.

'The captain has gone into the mountains in search of a river.'

'When will he be back?' I asked.

He looked at me and smiled.

'Who knows. He has been gone a week, so far. He might be somewhere over here,' prodding the map. 'I'll be surprised if he ever returns.'

'I have to go back on the stores,' I said.

'You have a farm don't you Ruse, thirty acres of it.'

'And you have a farm three times the size, but are eating off the stores.'

He stood up, angry, shouting.

'Do not be bloody impertinent with me. You were given the land so you could be off the stores. You and others.'

'My wife is with child, due not more than a month away, and she is bony when she should be full.'

'In the absence of Captain Tench, I'd say a decision to put you back on the stores would be a decision for the governor.'

'Will you ask him?' I pleaded.

'When I next see him.'

The stream we drank from died. Redcoats were sent into the woods with barrels to find another and defend it; river water was boiled and cooled. Birds, bats and men fell to the ground, one man on my land. When we lifted him to the graveyard he weighed no more than a sheep. I stopped work, sent men from my farm until the drought ended. We took sick, Elizabeth and me. Blood poured out of me, all my lower body gone red, weeks of headaches. Elizabeth was all bone and sallow. Her middle rounded but shrunken, not plump like Susanna was. She would lay her eyes half-closed, her palms resting and nigh on covering her swell.

'James, I wondered last night, that if I lose this child, whether I'd be able to carry another. I always thought my mother would be with me when the time came, that I'd be on the farm. Mother and my aunts all around me. But here we are.'

She held out a hand, I took its lightness in mine.

'James, do you think this place really wants us, our child? I have such dark thoughts and I cannot be this weak, not at this time.'

Next morning, I fetched the woman Martha, and I went back to see the sergeant who had refused me food.

'Can I have a rifle for a few hours?'

His eyes put a question to me.

'To hunt. I am a free man, I am allowed to hunt game, I just don't have anything to do it with. I have a child due and my wife needs meat. That's all.'

He gave me the Brown Bess in the corner, opened a drawer, and handed me three cartridges and a tin of powder. The barrel was long, up to my waist. I examined the brass workings above the trigger. He waved his hand for me to leave.

'I want it back here by sundown.'

My feet were nailed to his floor.

'I ain't never used one before sir.'

He snatched it off me; put his other hand out for a cartridge.

'Come with me,' he commanded.

I followed him to the edge of the woods. He held the musket up to my eye-line.

'Pull this back, half-cock. Bite off the top of the cartridge, pour in the powder, the wad and the ball. Ram it home with the rod. Put a pinch of powder in your pan. Pull the cock back, fire it at something.'

We could hear the bird call that sounded like a wheelbarrow wanting oil. He tugged the butt into his shoulder, swept the barrel in an arc, until he saw the bird with the shape of a jackdaw and the colouring of a magpie. He fired and it spun down to the dust below.

'They look a lot better than they taste. Two shots left.'

I had been into the woods west of my land on occasions, a mile at the most. I liked to wander in the woods at home. It was a place to dream. In the woods of New Holland I felt as I did in England when I was out poaching at night, more frightened with each step. I headed for a pond I knew a quarter of a mile in. If there was any water left in it there might be game. At first the woods were thin, a scattering of twisted grey stumps, the ground a blanket of bark and ash. Then the ground sloped away to a greener clough, with thickets and ferns. There was a riverbed, dry, that fed the pond, its rocky bottom was rust. There was a fallen tree and I lay behind it, rested my rifle on it, pointing at the pond below, which still had a low basin of water lying in it. The light was weak, it was approaching dusk, but there would be no sunset, just a thickening of the heat under cloud. This I knew, was the time when New Holland creatures awoke and came into the open. I rolled onto my back and primed the rifle as the officer had showed me, and left it at half cock. I practiced taking aim, squinting down the length of the barrel to one rock or branch after another. I had never fired a gun before, never held one. I remembered one September evening in Cornwall, with my brother, scrumping an orchard. We'd been at it all week, by the Friday we were on our last tree mostly taking windfall when I heard a thud like an axe against wood, and then a scream from my brother. He was on his knees crying, 'James, James, help me. Fetch father.'

I half dragged him into the woods and lay down next to him as he cried into fallen leaves. His backside and his back had buckshot in them, and a doctor came to our house to take them out, even though we hadn't sent for him and my father couldn't pay him. He said he would come back in a week, told us not to worry about payment, and not to speak of it to anyone.

I woke to the beat of wings and saw one duck chase another across the pond. I lifted my rifle and steered it to follow the second duck. I pulled the lever back full-cock and was about to fire when the soft brown background jumped away to one side. I lifted my head and saw the kangaroo, come to drink. It was a fortnight or more of meat. It hunched, tucking up its front legs, and before dipping to the water, looked over to me. Then it gently folded itself down to the water showing me its rump. I pulled the trigger, the long barrel jerked up, a crack rang out that Elizabeth would have heard, and I couldn't see ahead for smoke. My prey was on the ground, its head in the pond. I walked over thinking I would come home like a hunter, a beast over my shoulders. Then suddenly it was up, dragging itself away from me. It took a bound but didn't land well. I could see that I had hit its haunch. I reloaded, all the time watching the animal jump and sway, unable to understand why its left leg wouldn't hold it up anymore. I quickly pushed down the ramrod, shouldered my rifle, and looked for my kangaroo. It was further down the slope, on the edge of the dry river, fifty yards away, lying on its side with a spear deep into it, a native boy standing over it. There were four of them, two teenagers, two men, one of them the leader with the in-turned foot. The teenager by the kangaroo shouted something at me, twice. It may have been a question, or a warning. Then he pulled his spear out of the animal's side, it shuddered for a few seconds. He repeated the word, the spear above his head. Their leader said something to him and repeated it. I didn't know if he wanted him to put the spear down or throw it at me. I shot him, shot the boy, the musket ball entering his chest and knocking him off his feet. They ran to him and I ran away, up the slope, through the burnt ground, the twisted trees, back to my farm.

I looked in my house and Elizabeth glanced across at me with raised eyebrows. I shook my head and went to the officers' quarters. Captain Tench had returned, and he was pointing his baton at the map which was now on the wall. The sergeant was stood to attention.

'Here's your musket sir.'

'Any luck Ruse?' clipped the sergeant.

'No sir. None'

'Then I'll have the cartridges back.'

He placed his palm in front of me.

'I used the cartridges sir, just didn't hit anything.'

'What in the bloody hell were you aiming at man?'

'Ducks sir.'

Tench was studying me. His face was grubby, scratched. It was a pinched face to begin with but it was thinner, and his uniform was coated in muck and dust. He looked like one of the men on his hulk. I didn't want to ask in front of that sergeant, but the truth is we were starving.

'Sir, I wanted to ask.'

'What Ruse?'

'I was trying to hunt today sir because...'

The sergeant butted-in over me.

'He wants to go on the stores sir. His wife is going to have a sprog.'

Tench looked at the sergeant and sighed.

'Give me the key sergeant, and put him in the ration book will you.'

He took me to the stores there and then, and gave me a week's ration.

I was planting maize when my child was born. I had cleared getting on to twelve acres of my thirty. I'd grubbed-up the trees, roots pulled out, not just leaving the stumps which would have meant wasting a tenth of every acre. I burnt the wood and dug in the ashes, then hoed it all up, doing eight or nine rods a day. Hard as nature was in New Holland I was ashamed for having to rely on the stores after all the land given to me. So my own farm would not be like the government farm, just scratched over. My own farm would be properly done. After digging in the ashes, I clod-moulded it, dug in the grass and weeds, and it was I reckon equal to ploughing. Then I let it lie as long as I could, exposed it to air and sun, and just before I sowed my seed I had turned it all up afresh.

The old woman Martha came walking towards me, looking at the ground as she went.

'You have a daughter, Mr Ruse,' she said.

'Is she well?' I asked.

'They are both weak, and the child should have more weight, but it is breathing well enough.'

Susanna couldn't stop smiling at our first born, Elizabeth. Now my wife Elizabeth held our baby and looked so forlorn. I went over and sat on the bed, she pulled me to her holding my neck tightly. We called our daughter Rebecca after her mother. Williams brought Elizabeth berries that Binda had picked, and though she was a little suspicious Elizabeth ate them.

As the weeks passed they both gained strength. The drought ended and there was something to harvest. I prayed for forgiveness for killing the boy and asked myself what Tench would do with me if I told him, how the natives would mark the boy's death. One morning about a month after I'd killed the boy I heard gunfire from the settlement farm. Gunfire like there was a battle. I told Elizabeth to stay in our house and went to look. Three convicts were dead on the ground, speared. Redcoats were running towards the river. McIntyre was looking down studying the face of one of the dead; an officer kicked him out of the way.

'McIntyre, what happened here?' I asked.

'Never seen the like of it in my life. Six of them here, bold as you like, throwing spears. That big black bastard with the gammy foot, he put two of them through those poor bastards, but then here's the thing, a redcoat put a ball into his side, and he went to the ground. The lad was walking over to him, fixing his bayonet to finish him when the bastard got to his feet and ran off. They're after him now.'

It was payback for what I had done, but I had not been punished. My guilt only grew. It took me back to the pond in the woods. It was full and the river into it flowing. I sat and waited for a judgement, but none came. No natives nor creatures. Judgement for me would come later.

At harvest time, Captain Tench came to my farm with his notebook.

'Just wheat and maize then Ruse. Have you thought about a vineyard, tobacco?'

'No sir. I don't like to leave the path of certainty. It's only food I want to grow.'

I thought if Tench had a farm he would grow only roses and grapes and apples, expecting others to feed him.

'Once I have taken the harvest to the cove, I would come off the stores. My wife at Christmas,' I said.

'Yes, I wanted to speak to you about your wife. The governor has agreed to pardon her. First free woman in the colony, so I gather. The both of you then, free settlers now.'

I reached-out my hand, though he didn't seem sure, he shook it.

'You went out exploring then,' I said to him. 'Where did you get to?'

'Following the Hawkesbury River, on foot this time.'

'What is it like, this river?'

'Large indeed. High gorges to wide plains. Still to be charted.'

I was thankful to him, Elizabeth not so. She reminded me of Will Bryant. You could give them the rest of the world to walk in, but they would only ever be free at home.

Rebecca took her first steps through my wheat field, holding her mother's hands whilst I played peak-a-boo with her. It was one of the few days I remember the child laughing, and the last before she fell into a fever. She fought it, coughing and sweating away for nearly a month, more asleep than awake until she was finally at peace. I wanted to bury her on my land but Elizabeth would not have it. So we laid Rebecca in the settlement graveyard that was growing by the day. All that night we lay awake.

'I have to tell you something,' I said. 'I killed this native boy, when I had the rifle. I didn't mean to.'

'Boy? How old was he, do you think?'

'I don't know. Sixteen, maybe.'

'And why are you telling me this now?'

'I've been wondering, if this is God's punishment for doing that?'

'Does God give a damn about the natives? They don't believe in him do they?'

'God cares about all living things,' I said.

'You think he cares about us, out here? I think we are too far away from him.'

'We're not. Can't ever be.'

She swung her legs off the bed and sat up.

'I don't want to have another child here, knowing it might not live. If we're both supposed to be free, then let us go home. You own this land, you can sell it. Then we won't have to work our passage home, we can pay for it.'

And I agreed.

CHAPTER 19

Homeland

1794 and the Hawkesbury River

I left nothing in the ground, not a stalk of wheat or maize, I sold it all putting nothing in the barn, nor keeping any seed for the following year. I would not need it, for we had decided to go back to England. It was eight years since I had been taken from her, sent to turn the soil of New Holland, and I expected that back in England life would have only become harsher. With the sale of my harvest and my land I hoped I'd be able to buy a small farm, though there was a war with France now, which would have only raised the price of land. Captain Tench and the governor had both returned; no doubt to do their duty. More convicts were being pardoned, given land, even Williams and McIntyre had thirty acres each. Some were settling; some were looking to work their passage home. Many would be press-ganged when they got there. Redcoats too were being given land, thirty acres, a hundred acres. Rose Hill was growing north and south of the river. So much land was being taken and sold, sometimes for no more than a bottle of rum, it made it seem an unimportant thing, when back home men were hanged for taking a pheasant from what was once common land.

Some of my grain I sold to the stores at Rose Hill, some at the cove and I went with it on a new schooner, filling the deck with sacks of wheat and taking half the time the *Lump* did.

'You know you can take it all by cart now. They've finished the road,' said the pilot.

'I like the river,' I said to him.

'Fine if you got the time.'

'I have,' I said.

I wondered about Susanna, for if she was still alive I would have two wives when I got to England and I thought I might have to change my name. Richard, my son, would be nine, going on ten-years-old and I was sure my father would've looked after him, most likely would have him reciting Psalms by now. I would have much to tell Richard, and a new mother for him to meet.

My grain was unloaded by convicts, the harbour master cursing them. I went to the stores office for payment. A clerk, not in uniform, stamping documents, spoke slowly and quietly to me, as if I was a fool.

'A price of five shillings a bushel has been agreed,' he said.

He was a gentlemen convict, like Charles Peat, given some office because of his education, believing I had none.

'Agreed by who?' I asked. 'I have to agree, don't I, otherwise it ain't an agreement.'

He folded his arms and leaned back in his chair.

'Tell me who else is going to buy it from you? It wasn't even your land until two years ago.'

'That may be, but the harvest hasn't been good has it? Which always puts up the price of grain.'

'If this was a market it would, but it isn't. If you don't agree with five shillings, then it'll be taken from you for nothing at all.'

'Not by you it won't,' I said. 'You're still a convict.'

He shoved a document and pen across the desk, I signed for the price of the twenty bushels I'd brought that day. He tried to sweeten things.

'How many bushels will you have?' he asked.

'Five hundred, maybe.'

'That's a sum of money. What will you do with it?'

'Buy land in England.'

'You won't get as many acres for it, I can tell you.'

'I want to sell my land as well. How do I do that?'

'I can have a notice drawn-up. How many acres do you have?'

'Thirty, nearly half of it cleared and fertile.'

'I don't know what you'll get for it, land is being given away, and there's convicts to clear it.'

I was paid in notes I could exchange for goods, some English coin, and Spanish pieces of eight. I walked away with more money in my pocket than I'd ever seen.

Sydney Cove was looking like it wanted to be a town but could not yet afford it. There were two wharves built and store houses as well. What it didn't have was ships in the harbour. I walked the rocks and where there once were tents there were now streets and houses, cobbles and brick buildings. There was a hospital and a school and there was rats. I came across the reverend's church, of wattle and daub with a thatched roof. I saw a wooden building that was no smaller than the church that called itself a theatre. There were other men, not redcoats, not convicts, talking on the street, smoking a pipe; and there were some stores, saying *General Provisions* and *Clothes Men and Women*. I walked in one and was met with the smell of tobacco and piss, though looked about and couldn't see why. There was one long table of goods: smocks, shirts, trousers, boots – all black, some hats, belts, and laces. This was their stall. There was only one window and it wasn't easy to see the things they had. A man behind the table greeted me, 'Good day, sir.'

A woman with a face of stone was sweeping the floor. They either needed more stock or a smaller store. Someone laughed loudly from outside the back, the woman stamped on something with the heel of her boot. I picked up a cap, coarsely woven, tried it on for size.

'How much is this?' I asked.

'Depends what you have to give me,' he said. 'Shilling coin or quarter ounce tobacco, some pork or beef, rum if you have any.'

'I can offer you a shilling,' I said.

He turned his head slightly as if he hadn't heard me right. I walked over and put the coin in his hand. His wife, I took her to be, stopped sweeping whilst I handed him the money.

'Is there anywhere I can buy my wife a dress?' I asked.

The woman ran over to behind the table and through a door, coming back with an armful of garments. Coloured cotton dresses.

'These came from a Dutch merchant. Nothing as light as these to be had in Sydney.'

'White don't stay white long do it,' I said.

I brought to mind Elizabeth's hair.

'You don't have red do you?'

'I think sir, with red, there is always a danger that a woman might give the wrong impression. How about green?'

She unfolded a green dress from the pile. It was dark, like the wattle leaf, with buttons along one side under the arm, and a cord about the waist.

'The merchant told us it was the fashion in Holland,' said her husband.

More laughter and shouting this time, from out the back. I paid him with my Spanish dollars, his wife wrapped Elizabeth's dress. I touched my cap to them, about to leave, the man asked, 'Fancy a taste of rum?' Before I said either way, he waved his hand, I followed him out of the back door into a yard where there were stools and barrels, two redcoats sitting, cups in hand. I was poured a tot into a tin. One redcoat grinned at me as I sat, two teeth in his head.

'Bought something have you?'

'I bought a dress for my wife.'

'Oh that's nice that is.'

'Nice indeed,' said the other, so hunched his head was near his table.

They laughed and poured themselves another measure of the drink, rum-coloured, sour as cud. The first one, he would not let the subject lie.

'Must have cost you a few pennies.'

'You a merchant then?' asked the other.

'No, a farmer.'

'One of the free-settlers are you?' asked the first, the toothless man.

'I am,' I replied, finishing the drink in two mouthfuls.

Their questions came at me more quickly.

'Must have come in on that ship, few months back then?'

'No, I was here from the beginning.'

I got up but the hunched redcoat was on his feet and upright, and in my road. The other, moved behind me, put his hand on my collar, his voice in my ear.

'A convict, a thief, given land. That's you is it? Tell me, why did they ship you out here? Wasn't for ploughing dirt was it?'

He pushed the point of a knife against my back, until I arched forward onto my toes.

'I stole watches,' I confessed.

He dug the tip of his blade into me. I let out a cry, almost a scream. I held my breath, my mouth open. He did not push it any further, but held me there.

'And now you're buying dresses for a whore wife.'

The other redcoat fleeced me of my coin, pushed me back to the store. I stood there a moment, then fell to my knees, groaning. The woman came over and gave me a handkerchief. She put a hand under my arm and helped bring me to my feet. Blood dripped onto the floor.

'Best be on your way, my dear.'

I walked back to the church, hand on my back, a burning spreading across my body.

The church itself was a long, low building with a squat tower. There was sawdust in the porch and in the nave, where the reverend was teaching a class of children, all sat on the floor. I held up my bloodied hand for him to see, he sent a boy to fetch his wife who came and took me to their house where she dressed the wound, binding a bandage right round my waist.

'Some will do a lot worse than this for a mouthful of grog,' she said. 'Drink has got its feet under the table in this town, and the people who should be seizing it, the redcoats, they are the worst with it.'

'They took my money from me, that I earned for selling my grain.'

'All of it?'

'Just the coins.'

'You get a good look at them?'

'As Will Bryant used to say, one lobster back looks the same as the next.'

I was fed and invited to stay. The reverend's adopted native girl, Araboo, recited the Lord's Prayer to our applause and we sang a hymn. The singing was joyful, not like on the hulk where we sang as slaves. When a gaol makes its convicts sing, it is not for the good of their souls, but for the good of its own conscience. In the morning, the reverend showed me around his kitchen garden.

'Look at this James, isn't it a miracle?'

He rested an unripe orange in his palm, then gently let its stem take the weight once more. It would grow to be the fruit we were given at The Cape, its tree like a small plum, but with green leaves not bronze.

'The seeds I got from our stay at Rio. I plan to have a row of them.'

He'd pruned the slender trunk to force the tops, had half an acre of pear and apple, a vineyard too. I'd always thought him a better gardener than Dodd, and wished I had the freedom to grow delights. He showed me the grave of his stillborn son, knowing my little Rebecca had died inside a year.

'Elizabeth now longs to leave New Holland, so I'm selling my crops and land.'

'You must pour out your sorrows before the Lord, James. Seek his mercy and compassion, and eventually he will render your reward. He has made our coming and our lives here a trial for a reason. That we may be better able to make a country fit for him. I know Rebecca passed without a baptism, for which I am sorry. This last year, I have been so occupied with building the church.'

A passenger helped the pilot row the schooner part of the way upriver to Rose Hill.

'This is a dog of a river,' said the pilot.

'Too shallow for a bigger boat I'd say,' said I.

'When they open-up the other river, I'll be away there. A boat can sail it.'

'What other river?'

'To the north,' he said pointing to the far bank.

'The one they call the Hawkesbury?'

'Aye, that's the one.'

I took the rest of my grain to Sydney by cart and waited for someone to buy my land. Each day I walked out to look at it, always contemplating about what needed to be done, then realising it was a waste of my thoughts. I went to help Williams with his plot. So much woods had been cleared I was stood on his land looking at the pond where I'd shot the kangaroo. And the native boy. Trees were dragged away and piled up around the sawpit that couldn't keep time with the axe. There was no method to Williams' farming. He'd move from one task to another before either of them were done, he sowed his maize amongst his wheat, was more interested in the woods at the end of his land than turning his soil. Binda lived with Williams in his hut but foraged for food elsewhere, bringing back more fruit and yams than he grew. They had grown filthy and lugged a stench about with them.

It was the same time of year near to the same date that Rebecca was born, two years after that I came back to my house to find the Rose Hill surgeon, Harris, standing outside with Elizabeth.

'This is the surgeon, James.'

'I know who he is.'

'Well he'd like to buy our farm,'

It was my farm. I walked him away from Elizabeth.

'How much are you prepared to pay?'

'Fifty pounds.'

'I got more than twice that from this year's harvest alone, and it was a poor one.'

'Your wife tells me you want to go home. The new governor is giving officers land, hundred acres a time. He would give me the same if I asked him. No-one else will buy it Ruse. You have more than enough to go home.'

Then he held out his hand for me to shake. I looked back at Elizabeth. She was leaning in our doorway, her eyes shut, dreaming of what I wondered. I shook his hand and we went to an office where I was given a note to exchange for fifty pounds of goods.

I got back to the house, pushed Elizabeth over a chair, and slapped her backside.

'I should take a strap to your back,' I said. 'Telling him how you wanted to go back to England. What do you think that did to the price? You're a stupid mare, girl.'

'We've been waiting and waiting haven't we?'

'He would've paid more.'

'No James, he only bought it because I told him that I wanted to go home. He wouldn't have bought it otherwise. Felt sorry for me he did.'

'He bought it because I have already worked the land for him. And he got it cheap. We could have waited.'

'We can't. I'm having another baby, and I won't see it die here. Least now we have money to get home.'

I wanted the child, I wanted children but we had no land, nowhere to live, no passage home. A child born at sea, it happens I thought. They survive.

I gave my hens to Williams and we took what we could carry to Sydney Cove the next day. We took lodgings in the brickmaster's house and I went to ask about the two ships that were in the harbour. One was a Spaniard, the other Dutch. The harbour master scratched his beard.

'Nothing dallies here for long. The Poder. She's setting sail end of the week.'

He stepped behind a broad book on the counter and placed his finger on a column. I leaned over and tried to read what was written, he closed the book on me.

'The Americas. California. She'll be going round The Horn, if you fancy that.'

'What about the Dutch ship?'

'He hasn't made up his mind.'

'Where can I find the captain?'

'On his ship.'

At the top of the gangplank was a man with a breastplate and sword. He had one foot on the threshold, one hand on his sword. I had to ask twice before he took me to his captain.

'I go to Batavia.'

'When will you be in Holland?'

'Long time.'

'Are there any women aboard?'

'Couple of whores, why?'

'My wife's with child.'

'She could have the child in Batavia. But, I don't want the life of an infant in my hands. Why not stay here?'

I went back to the harbour master. There were no ships expected, but then there never was, they arrived out of nowhere, so little of the world knowing we were there. Few words passed between Elizabeth and me. We sat in our room listening to Bloodworth, the brickmaster cursing the laziness of convicts. My land had been taken, my house too, my freedom gone again before I'd barely tasted it. I was being transported back to England. That was how it seemed. Bloodworth carried on with it whilst we were in bed, I said to Elizabeth, 'My child will not be born at sea. They have less chance of surviving there, you as well. Not in the America's either, or some foreign port. You are my wife and you will do as I tell you. I have to go to Rose Hill. From there I will find somewhere else for us. Until I return I want you to stay here. Stay close to the brickmaster's wife, understand?'

'When will you be back?'

'A week or so.'

I asked the sergeant if he knew anyone who had been to the Hawkesbury by foot.

'They've all left. Tench, the governor, Bradley, Dawes, gone back to England. The natives that went with them, they're still here, if you can find them.'

They would never lead someone like me there; they understood rank as well as any Englishman.

'How far to the Hawkesbury?' I asked.

The sergeant turned to the map on the wall.

'This far. Thirty miles perhaps. Ridges, gorges, you couldn't do it.'

'But they did it.'

'They are marines, Ruse. Officers, nearly all of them.'

Yet not one of them a farmer, who must walk miles and haul stone and earth every day of the year. The sergeant went on, 'And the natives, they can walk over one horizon after another.'

He stepped over to the open door.

'Wait.'

He went outside, yelling at a private.

'Cohen! Cohen! Haul yourself here lad.'

Cohen was stout, flabby in a colony of the half-starved.

'Tell Ruse how you got to the Hawkesbury.'

'Six days march.'

'You bloody fool! The route.'

He dragged the private over to the map, but he could make no sense of it. He strode outside.

'That way,' he pointed, 'until you come to a hill with no trees, then go right. Any water you come across, walk downstream. It all flows into the big river.'

'How will I know the Hawkesbury?'

'Because you will not be able to cross it. Sir, have I to go again?'

'No, but Ruse, you'd be a fool to go alone,' said the sergeant.

I didn't go alone, I took Williams and Binda who didn't give it a second thought and went to begin walking off the moment I asked them. The sergeant gave me Cohen's kitbag. I brought a gun and some food and carried a bedroll, a pan, what water I could. Williams and Binda brought and carried nothing. Cohen took us to where he had begun with Tench, and I could see a marked way at the start, but we lost it after half a mile.

'Binda, you know the big river in the north?' I asked pointing.

'Deerubbin? I never been. Catta people.'

Me and Williams took this to mean another tribe. It was the hottest time of the year and for the first two days the walk was mostly uphill though not steep. The undergrowth was thick and we had to walk round it rather than through it, making our way up country only in great slow loops. Binda slept soundly on rock, Williams also. To stop myself being bitten, I would roll myself in my blanket like it was a shroud, only finding sleep when utterly spent. Our water was gone in a day, but before we set down each night Binda would dig a hole that would fill with water by morning. Then she bailed out the dirty water and slowly the hole would fill with water we could drink. By the third day, we were walking aside streams all day. I didn't use my musket for food at first, Binda and Williams dug-up wild potatoes that grew shallow in the ground. Six of them boiled would be enough for a meal. There was fruit and she and Williams ate ants and grubs, which I wouldn't. We came across the remains of a campfire and Binda cried, 'English fire.'

A mile later, she said, 'Catta people land.'

I didn't know if we should be afeared or not. Catta land was wet, the ground springy, water lying under the grass swelling it into tussocks.

There were unseen ditches to break a leg in, no step even with the last. Ducks flew over our heads due north. The land was more open, but the plentiful water meant we could no more walk straight than when we were in the thickness of the forest. The ground became a bog, penned in by two small rivers. It was like this for more than a day, until we followed them into the one river. We followed this downstream and came upon a native spearfishing, the tallest man I ever saw. He had a necklace of duck feathers and I approached like he was just another Cornishman.

'Deerubbin?'

He pointed ahead, replying in words I was unable to repeat. I asked Binda to act as a go-between, but she was afeared of him. He came over to me demanding something; I remained steadfast.

'He wants gift from you. He will take us to Deerubbin if you give him something.'

We didn't need him to find north, but I opened my kitbag and gave him my blanket. He jigged about for a moment. I tied the blanket round his neck and he wore it like a cape, leading us on, carrying his spear.

'Binda, Binda. Ask him how far.'

Another day's walk. We camped at a bend in our river that we knew was draining into the Hawkesbury. Our guide caught fish, only a mouthful or two each. Binda rubbed the oil on herself, so did Williams.

'It stops you being bitten.'

'I'd sooner be eaten than smell like you John.'

From out of the dark, there came voices, a woman's song, and another man, calling from the water. They had more food and showed not the smallest interest in me or Williams. I took it that these people knew of the English, but must not have seen the pox, or have heard of the killing; the towns built at Sydney Cove and Rose Hill. Either that or they were a most forgiving people. We were ferried across the little river in their canoe, the bog becoming a plain. A place of bright, even grassland. I could not yet see the Hawkesbury but I knew it was there, the earth under my feet put there by the river. The land fell away, trees began to lean forward, there was the smell after a tide has gone out. We came upon it, lying quiet and deep, a pair of black swans upon it, and so broad it could only be crossed by a great bridge. We lay down upon its bank.

I rose and dug into the soil with my bayonet, the guide beseeching me for the weapon, I denied him. The soil was a light, rich mould, about the banks timber that the river had left there. I looked about for higher ground and half-a-mile downstream, where it forked, I found a raised bank some thirty feet above the silver water. I climbed up to it and but for flowers the land was clear. I saw in my mind a field. I could make a farm without slaves. I would buy more seed and I would have a harvest by the time of my next child. Before then, I would hunt and gather wild potatoes. I would bring wheat and vegetables with me.

'Binda, how far to the sea? Ask our friend.'

Three days, maybe less by boat. There would be no convicts to steal the crops; so few of us, we would not rile the natives. In time, a boat would come to buy my grain.

I took the guide with me to shoot a kangaroo. This time I brought down a small one that, with a musket ball in its behind, struggled to get back to its feet. The guide speared it dead and skinned it; I butchered it for the fire.

'John, I think we should settle here. The land looks good. We're a long way from redcoats and convicts.'

'You don't want to go back to England?'

'I might someday, but Elizabeth is with child again. Would you settle here?'

'If that's what you want.'

John Williams never had his own path and was happy to follow mine. He asked Binda to ask our friends what they thought about us living next to Deerubbin.

'He wants your musket.'

'He can have it.'

We returned to Rose Hill and Williams put his farm up for sale. I told Elizabeth where we were going.

'You will be a farmer's wife, you hear. Not some man without land to his name. My children will have land.'

'You can do this? Just go somewhere and start digging-in, you don't have to ask no-one?'

'I asked some natives.'

'You asked the governor yet? How do you know it will be yours to keep?'

I had to tell my tale to three other men before I could stand face-to-face with Governor Grose.

'Where on the Hawkesbury?' he asked, putting a map in front of me.

'I don't know exactly sir. The native guide said it was three days walk to the sea, and the land was flat either side of the river.'

'Here, beyond the mountains. You walked from Rose Hill?'

'Yes sir. And I wish to pay for a boat to take me there, with some provisions to start a farm.'

'Just you?'

'My wife also. And John Williams and his woman.'

'You say the soil is good there?'

'And the land without woods. Grassland.'

'Tell me, how wide is the river along there?'

'A hundred feet wide or more.'

'I'll see to the boat, but there needs to be more of you if you want to survive.'

Williams got twice as much for his land as I did for mine and when he arrived at the cove he had McIntyre with him. We set-off up the coast in a twenty-foot cutter, its pilot the man who had taken my grain from Rose Hill to the cove. Along the coast north, the surf raged against the cliffs. There was no shelter for us until we reached Broken Bay, the river's estuary, where we struggled a long while to enter against the tide. Whilst we had light, we made for the nearest beach. There were lights from native fires so we crept past them on the water and landed further along under darkness. In the morning there were women about us catching crayfish. I noticed something that I had seen before, seen on Binda: part of the little finger on the left hand was missing, as if it had been cut away at the second joint. The women were friendly but their men came asking for our clothes. We were away in the cutter quickly, the pilot heading for a channel on the north side of the bay that was the river's course. There were two days of winding one way then another, all of us rowing in turn for between the high hills there was little wind. By the evening of the second day we were leaving the mountains behind, but we could not tell what the country was outside of the river, for we were beneath the tree-lined banks. Every hour or so, the pilot brought her to a bank and I would climb up to view the land. We came to a bend where a smaller river forked away south and the bank was high and steep. From the top, I could see a lush plain on all sides. I breathed in deeply and called down, 'This is it. Yes, this is the place.'

CHAPTER 20

The Beast of the Field

We laid out our lands in a row, three acres across. Mine, tucked into the corner at the river's fork, with water on two sides, then Williams' and McIntyre's plots. We did not think of marking borders for we could farm back as far as we liked, there being a plain of open ground behind us. McIntyre and me, we had brought tents with us, Williams had not thought to do so, so he and Binda slept with us. This was of comfort to Elizabeth for we were quite alone, and Binda, who she once took as an enemy, she now saw as protection from other natives. Goodwill with the natives was important for we had nothing to give them. We had only tools for ourselves with no stores to turn to. The boat that had brought us promised to return in a month to keep us provided; the governor had seen to that. He wanted another settlement in the colony, while I wanted away from convicts and redcoats. I had my vegetables in the ground a week after the tents were up, preparing the soil taking no time at all. More and more every day we had the attention of natives.

There was a group of a half-dozen who lived on the banks aside our huts, living on what we thought was our land. The man who had brought us there I came to know him as Yellowgowie. He was the highest ranking in the group. With Binda's help, I tried to show him how to cultivate the land. Whilst it was something he had an interest in, it was not such that he wanted a farm of his own. Indeed, I soon took it that the land I was digging, that any of us were digging, he thought as his. Whatever claims I made to it, whatever piece of paper given to me, he would never think any different. When the boat came the following month, it brought more provisions for us and it also brought more settlers. Another half-dozen plots along the south bank of the river, stretching as far back as they pleased. They did not seem like lawless people; they were young farmers, one of them a Methodist, but all had muskets, a few, cutlasses too. The pilot said they were free-settlers.

'They're coming on the same ships as the convicts. More of them every time. I have documents for all of you.'

It was a land grant of thirty acres.

'There's one for all of you, and there'll be more to follow. They're building a bigger boat to get people up here.'

Most nights we had a campfire, usually by my hut, and I was pleased that there were women who would be able to be with Elizabeth when her time came. I asked one of the settlers what news there was from England.

'A bloody war with France. The French are fighting in Austria, and will invade England if they can. Men are enlisting or else press-ganged everywhere. Some think war's a fine sport, but not me. My harvest wouldn't pay the rent on my farm, so when we heard there was land for the taking here I thought I'd spread my wings.'

I realised by the looks alone he was a little wary of me because I was a convict, that my time being done made no difference to him.

'You don't mind them on your farm then, the natives?' the settler asked.

'I'd rather they kept away, but they're not going to, and I don't want trouble with them. My wife pregnant 'n all.'

'What do they want from us?' he asked me.

'Clothes, tools, and they like the maize, and they will take it,' I said.

'Well, if they take mine, there will be trouble.'

His name was Doyle and we went out hunting duck together. His father had taught him how to shoot well, until the day he was hanged for poaching. Doyle saw the land differently to those of us who had been sent to dig it as a punishment. He had crossed the oceans to possess it and everywhere he walked he seemed to covet the ground, many times saying to me, 'The fields here James, they don't have an end. Who's to stop us taking what we want?'

My son came into this world at harvest time. We called him James. When Elizabeth was back on her feet, Doyle, McIntyre, Williams, they came to our hut to shake our hands and share a little food. We were all standing about outside when Elizabeth took fright, pointing toward the open land behind the farms. A group of natives were walking our way carrying spears. There were no women amongst them, no children. One of their sand coloured dogs circled them. We gathered our muskets and readied them with shot. They came right up to us, unafraid, for they are all that way. Amongst them was Billy, the boy taken in by Surgeon Harris at Rose Hill. He had grown some, a strong looking lad now with pipe clay across his face. His English was good, he wore breeches and a coat, and he spoke on behalf of all of them.

'I'm Young Billy, this is Yellowgowie. You all coming, building huts here, without asking, like Parramatta. You don't ask. You have to give hatchets, if you stay here.'

'We got nothing to spare,' said Doyle.

And we hadn't. But anything at all would have done, would have been wise.

'We need to give them a gift,' said Binda.

Doyle spat on the ground, repeating loudly, 'Nothing to give.'

Young Billy walked up to Doyle.

'You see what you want and take it.' He felt Doyle's waistcoat. 'This for Yellowgowie.'

Doyle shoved him away and brandished his musket. Yellowgowie had seen me use mine and did not raise his spear. He threatened us in his tongue and they slowly returned along the smaller south leading river. Yellowgowie threw his spear far into the distance, Young Billy shouted back at us, 'This is not good, not law.'

'Bloody funny notion of the law,' said Doyle.

If we had given them something that day it would not have prevented what came to pass, but it would have seen away death for a time, some lives would have been longer.

A few days later, I was out hunting duck, splashing across the water-logged flats, when Yellowgowie and Young Billy walked across my line of sight. I called out to them and gave them a duck.

'Are you angry with me?' I asked Young Billy.

'Not angry with Ruse, with others.'

Yellowgowie waved his hand from side-to-side, saying, 'Deerubbin... Deerubbin.'

I didn't know what he meant, but musket or not he made me nervous. I walked away, up-river, shot some more duck. When I got home, Elizabeth wasn't there, our hut was broken and clothes and food had been taken. I found her at Williams' farm, lying on the bed in a disturbed state, James on her breast.

'Elizabeth?'

'Yellowgowie, Young Billy, went to your farm, stole your things,' said Williams.

'Did they touch her?' I asked.

'No,' he said.

'James?'

'Baba's fine.'

'Where are they now?'

'Gone.'

I put Elizabeth and baby James with Doyle, who I trusted with his rifle if they attacked his farm, then straightaway I went looking for them with mine. Two days I was gone. As far back as the bogland where we'd first met Yellowgowie. I found tracks and I saw a glimpse of one or two, but I never got a shot at him. This would be the way of it when redcoats went on a hunt after an attack. I came back up the river from the south, walked through my farm, and saw Young Billy sitting on the riverbank next to Williams. I laced right into him, boy as he was. I lifted him up, put my hands around his throat.

'Keep away from my farm, you hear? Tell Yellowgowie Ruse will shoot him with musket, with gooro-beera, if he comes frightening my woman and child again. Understand?'

Young Billy never made a sound; he took his beating without complaint. Williams watched on in silence, as he did most of the time, at most of the world. Yellowgowie, I never saw again, not until his dying day.

A bigger boat brought more settlers. They dug themselves in along the river as far as you could see, and they staked-off land behind us as well. On that boat was Charles Peat, the gentleman highwayman. He looked happier than I had seen him, his smile confident, speaking as he did when I first met him, like a prophet come among us.

'Tilling the land James, is for unknown heroes such as yourself, every one of you an Adam in Eden. A life not for me though, I am a man of commerce now.'

'You're making a living off a boat?'

'The colony is spreading its wings. Sydney town cannot feed itself, if it ever could. I am here to bring your food to its tables. They say this place will be the granary of the kingdom. Tell me, are the natives giving you any trouble?'

'Things are coming to a head with them.'

'You have the numbers here, surely.'

'We do. But that might also be the cause of it.'

'Our world depends upon the destruction of theirs. They know it, even if we do not.'

Peat went from farm to farm; selling clothes and tools for coin or an agreed price to take their grain to Sydney. He'd also brought rum with him, which men would trade their grain for, Williams more than most. He found a thirst for it and so did Binda, and she with child. Peat's boat came each month bringing more settlers, carpenters, and bricklayers to build homes. There were no redcoats at first, but the governor sent us a constable called Andrew Thompson, a Scot, and an ex-convict at that. He took up an acre behind my farm to build a house.

The growing ranks of settlers made us feel safer, they were a comfort to Elizabeth who was fretful day and night. But when the maize was ready, whole clans of natives, men, women and children came with nets to take the cobs. I saw the blanket I gave to Yellowgowie used to carry away the food I had grown. I fired into the air and they didn't flee, but only threw stones back. There were raids on crops at night, and a settler beyond Doyle's farm was speared through the shoulder. His spilt blood began a trail that soon ran all along the south side of the river.

A meeting was held at McIntyre's farm where people decided to organize patrols. McIntyre said he was drawing-up a petition, to give people permission to shoot natives if they came onto their land. No-one argued back. The next night we heard something from beyond Williams' farm: screams. I wasn't sure if it was man or bird. I looked out and could see a fire burning. I got up, lit a candle, and started loading my musket.

'What do you think you're doing, you're not the constable are you?'

'Someone could be in strife out there,' I said.

'You can't leave us here. I've already lost a daughter; I'm not losing a son to the savages.'

I stayed. Sitting outside the door with my Brown Bess loaded. I fell asleep, woken by the long thud of a gunshot. Dawn had set the river on fire. I went to Thompson's house, the constable. We walked over to McIntyre's farm to find him and Doyle sitting by smoking embers.

'Bit early to be out on patrol constable,' said McIntyre.

'Bit early to have your neighbours over, wouldn't you say?' said Thompson.

'We have to look after each other these days, don't we?' said Doyle.

I looked at the remains of the fire; there was a length of rope on the ground.

'People say they heard a commotion coming from here last night,' said Thompson.

'There was screaming,' I said.

'That was an owl,' said Doyle, to McIntyre's laughter.

'And gunfire,' I added.

'Well, I heard that too,' said Doyle, 'and I'm not surprised. Just before nightfall, your man Yellowgowie, and nine or ten others, were seen back there, waving spears. They looked ready to attack when I saw them. Could be one of my neighbours gave 'em a volley.'

Beyond the fire, I could tell something had been dragged to the river. I followed the marks. The morning sun was throwing stars on the water, but when I shaded my eyes I could see something bobbing to the surface with rope around it. It looked like a barrel. I waded-in, pulled it out of the water, up onto the bank. It was a native, trussed-up, hands tied to feet. It was Young Billy, his face knotted in agony, his eyes open. He'd been burned and shot. McIntyre and Doyle got to their feet; the constable cut the rope, the body stayed as it was, hunched-up and twisted. Doyle spoke for them both.

'He was spying for them, for Yellowgowie and the others. He was seen on the farm where the man was speared, the same day, offering to work for him. He was planning an attack.'

'So you killed him?' asked the constable.

'Didn't want to kill him,' said Doyle. 'He was on his way to signal the others, we had to stop him.'

'So you shot him while he was running off,' I asked, 'and then tied him up afterwards, did you?'

McIntyre and Doyle were taken to Sydney to face a court. Their neighbour, who had been speared in the shoulder, was later murdered with his wife and child. Crops were burned, farms raided, for maize, for livestock. Elizabeth despaired.

'You said it was safe here.'

'It was,' I replied, 'when we first came.'

'It isn't now. A family has been murdered. At Rose Hill it was just the redcoats that was speared. We could be next. Either we have to get out of here or the natives do.'

'I've had enough of starting again,' I said.

A week later, Constable Thompson was back with McIntyre and Doyle, and a party of redcoats.

'They made it sound like their lives were in danger. I told the court about the burns, saying I thought the boy had been tortured, but they both said he was calling for his mates when they shot him. McIntyre was fined for forging signatures on his petition. They left it at that.'

The redcoats had a barracks built, they were there to stay and they lapped-up Peat's rum. They patrolled the track between the farms and the riverbank where our fields ended. There was no parley, no meeting around a white flag, they opened fire if a corncob was taken. If there was a raid on a crop at night, they would go in search of natives the next day, finding no-one. I was harvesting the last of my maize when a woman and girl who had been crouching beneath my crop stood up. They ran, both with an armful of cobs. I didn't shout, but only sighed, thinking it would be the last of the pilfering for the year. The nearest redcoat was back on McIntyre's land. Then a distant slap and a puff of smoke from across the riverbank, the mother stumbled to the ground. I walked over slowly, unsure if the one had been the cause of the other. From out of the bushes across the river, a redcoat appeared, reloading his musket. I waved at him not to shoot. The woman was laying on her side, with a hole the size of a shilling into her ribs. The child, maybe ten-years-old, was standing above her, the cobs in her arms. There was no surgeon at the river to get the ball out. If it had been an arm or a leg she might have lived. She died the next morning, same place as she fell, having barely moved, only lifting her head for sips of water. Some natives came and made a ceremony, took her body away.

Yellowgowie came in the rain, the same evening. It was a torrent, and the pipe clay washed off his face and body as he walked slowly along the track, talking to himself. He was not carrying a spear, a stick instead, with its end shaped like a hatchet. The redcoat who had shot the woman had taken it upon himself to defend my farm. He was standing on the track at the top of my path like a sentry. Perhaps he felt guilt about shooting the woman, perhaps he didn't want to show any fear to the native man, but either way he unshouldered his musket too late and Yellowgowie struck him across his head, putting him on the ground, before walking down my path towards me. There was no time to get my gun, even to go into the hut and reach for a hatchet. He stopped a pace away from me and began telling me again and again, 'Deerubbin, Deerubbin, come, come, come.'

The redcoat got to his knees, wiped the blood from his eyes, and put a musket ball into Yellowgowie's back that passed through him and dug itself into my shoulder.

CHAPTER 21

The Deluge

The musket ball wasn't in me deep. I thought about taking it out myself, but my right arm had gone stiff and my left hand has always been a stranger to me. McIntyre offered to do the job. He had served he suddenly claimed, had been a soldier, had *seen wounds and borne wounds for many a year*. I knew him as someone untouched by others' pain, so I declined his generous offer. There was no-one along the river I trusted with a blade, so Surgeon Harris from Rose Hill was sent for, the man who had bought my land so cheaply. I believed him obliged to me and as such, I thought, would be bound to work on me carefully. He must have regretted taking-up farming for he took it out on my shoulder. I took rum for the pain while he dug into me, grateful that Williams had plenty to give me.

Grog houses were opening up along the river, people buying from Charles Peat and then selling it on by the cupful. McIntyre ran such a house and Williams and Binda idled their time there in a daze, their child at the same table. Williams ran up a slate at McIntyre's, promising more and more of his grain with every blind drunk day, until McIntyre realised that there would be no grain because the farmer was always drunk.

After Harris took out the ball, stitched and strapped me up, he asked to visit the grave of Young Billy. Thompson the constable had made McIntyre and Doyle bury Billy on the edge of his land, there being no graveyard at that time. He had not shown the body to Yellowgowie or the others, for he thought it would only have riled them more. There was a cross of branches, nothing more, so we cut and carved his name on some sandstone. Billy had been with the surgeon for going on three years, he had been a father to the boy.

'Billy was smart. He learned quickly. But not quickly enough it seems.'

Surgeon Harris was having a house built on my old farm, Rose Hill was now called Parramatta, the name the natives gave to the river there. I asked him if he would come to the Hawkesbury, for we needed a surgeon.

'This place is fast getting a reputation, for rum and lawlessness. We came to this land to grow something more than grain.'

I never touched a drop of grog beyond my surgery, but on the next farm grass was growing where there should have been wheat, Binda walked in circles muttering to herself, lost in dreams or sorrows.

We lived by the river for another three or four harvests. The natives subdued, we hardly saw them. We fed Williams and Binda for they would only have starved or walked into the woods and starved there. The river and the soil it had laid for us were kind, obedient, but all life turns against taming.

Before it came, there was the hail. But not like the small stones of England, and the sky was not pale grey but somehow green, like early wheat. The ice that fell, fell to us in broken pieces, cutting heads, shoulders, the backs of beasts and digging into the ground. It clattered against itself like shells in a bag. There followed a darkness, to the east and the west, leaving us in a well. When it came, it came not as a storm, for there was no wind, the air was still and trumpets of thunder did not announce the coming of the deluge, it came creeping upon us as slowly as autumn, each day a degree more severe than the last. The rain was slight at first, like an English April, flickering off the water, but it was ceaseless, getting thicker and faster until you couldn't tell the river from the sky. It would slow or it would hasten, be gentle or thrash us, but it did not stop, not for twenty days. When the ground was full to the brim, and the ducks preferred the fields to the river, the rain stopped and there was light in the well. I looked down from the end of my land to the quickening river below. The Hawkesbury had climbed but it was still yards beneath me, twenty feet or more. How could Deerubbin invade my farm? Doyle went off to shoot duck in the land behind us and came back saying it was a marsh now, *no difference between the creeks and the grass.* The river to the east of my farm, that forked into the Hawkesbury we had called South Creek, and it too took on a great rush, as if a multitude of other streams were emptying into the one and choking it. The natives could not boat in it, it was so fast, and it swelled the Hawkesbury. It did not rain on us, not for a week, but its mark we could see on the horizon, feeding the river, causing it to rise at the fork around my farm. Charles Peat came in his boat, with blankets and clothes to give, and rum to sell.

'The current coming out of Broken Bay was so strong the journey took us twice as long. The way home will take half the time. There is this rain everywhere and talk of high tides. All omens I think.'

There was a week of sunshine. Peat left us. Deerubbin began to fall away, a foot or more. It was the time to plant, but seeds rot in sodden ground, so we would have to wait. I believed the heavens had drained, but then clouds banked like a wall and this time rain pounded the earth, trying to break it open. It entered huts and houses. Roofs buckled beneath it and hens died under it. Some days you could not see a yard ahead of you. Thompson came to our hut.

'First sign of it easing, and I'm heading for Rose Hill. The river will come and take us away if we don't.'

Doyle went with him, but we stayed. So did Williams and Binda, McIntyre, all watching the sky every morning. The Hawkesbury was still three yards below the bank. Another three days, we couldn't light a fire, we went to McIntyre's; it was the same there. Next morning we all headed south for Rose Hill. After the first day, we could go no further, for the marsh that Doyle had spoken of had become a lake. We thought of going to the wilderness of higher ground, with the hope that natives would take us in, but they would have heard of the murders, and shunned us at the least. I prayed, asked the others to pray, and then we went back. When we got there, South Creek could no longer hold its water, had spilled it onto my land from upstream. The next day, beyond McIntyre's farm, the water found its way to the Hawkesbury from behind us, making our three farms an island. Williams stood there, turning full circle in the twilight, drinking his last bottle of rum. Elizabeth and me, we watched the deluge from our door.

There was no more than a sigh as Deerubbin reached for us. All in a moment, it was lapping about our waists. Elizabeth stumbled, I took James from her, the deluge swept on. We waded away from the river, looking over our shoulders as we went, lest another wave come for us. I heard a shout, I heard my name called.

'Hold on there, Ruse. Ruse, yer mad bastard.'

McIntyre, kneeling on the water, on a raft, with a paddle in his hands.

'I hated that lousy house anyway.'

He was rowing a wall of his hut. We put James on board and then lay upon it, keeping it steady as he steered it downstream. McIntyre had brought his musket and some rope with one end tied round his waist.

'I'd tie myself to a tree if I thought it wouldn't get torn out of the ground.'

The moon was cloud-masked but I could make out Williams' hut off to the left as we passed.

'What about Williams? They have a child,' I shouted.

'I went there, they've gone.'

'You sure?'

'No-one there.'

A current began to drag us, McIntyre stopped paddling, we held the sides of the raft. I looked behind me, a second wave was coming. It swept us ahead like a leaf on a stream, water lapping over us while we waved along. Half-a-mile further on we were beneath a higher bank, we scrambled up. The river had widened itself, had grown to twice its size, it was carrying trees, shrubs, huts and houses away with it. All things unwanted being driven towards the sea. I wondered at the redcoats in their barracks up-river. Maybe we should have paddled there, for where were we going downriver? Elizabeth got to her feet.

'James, it's Williams. Look, there!'

There was a door, a roof, turning on the water. Between a few pulled apart planks, a man was holding his head back, keeping his face out of the water, fighting the current no more than the wreckage.

'McIntyre, the rope. Williams!' I yelled.

McIntyre threw the rope downstream of Williams. We hauled him out. He didn't speak or look to any of us. He hung his head, trembling with the cold and with his loss. No-one asked about Binda or his child. Where had he been when McIntyre went to his hut? We stayed where we were until light, when we could not tell the river from the land. We talked about where we should go and how we could get there, our words having no clear course. We argued until we saw Charles Peat's boat crawl out from the horizon.

There were others on board who had been washed out. The Government in Sydney looked after us, clothed us, and housed us; they did it because they wanted us to go back and farm at the Hawkesbury.

'I'll do whatever you ask James,' Elizabeth said to me, sounding nothing like the woman I met at Rose Hill.

I was told I could have another thirty-acre grant of land, further away from the river, but I said nothing to Elizabeth. There was now a boatyard at the cove and I'd go and watch them working some days, it helped me forget the calamity that had befallen my hopes. One day I saw Thompson there, shaking hands with a man. I couldn't hear what was said for the shipwrights were riveting a hull. He took me to one side afterwards.

'That was the owner of the ship they're building. I'm going to charter it from him.'

'To go where?' I asked.

'Not so far. Down the coast from here.'

'To move settlers?'

He was being secretive, to make himself look more important, constables of the law like to do that. He went on.

'You took a boat up to Broken Bay didn't you? Did you look at the shoreline on the way, see the creatures on the rocks. Know what they were James?'

'Seals,' I said, like a schoolboy.

'*Sealskins*, James. Seals are clothed in money. They are there in their thousands and it is better to hunt them at certain times of the year, when they're breeding on the rocks and that time is approaching. I've got a captain, now I'm looking to crew the boat, to bring back a lot of skins.'

'I don't know about that kind of thing, I only know about farming.'

'Farming has been no friend to you James. You gave it your all but it has you wrung out. With the sealing, there isn't much to learn, you kill them, and then you skin them. But there is a certainty of reward.'

'How much money we talking about?'

'The skins you take will be worn round the necks of ladies in Paris. In two months, you'd make what a farmer with thirty acres makes in a year. And after a few voyages you'll be able to buy twice as much land wherever you like. Are you interested?'

'Perhaps I am, but why you asking me?'

'It's bloody work. You've killed animals haven't you? And it is hard work, you're a grafter. Plenty of men in Sydney can use a knife, but I need men I can trust not to put it in another man. I'll make sure your family's looked after while you're away. Sailor's wives stay close to one another.'

I spoke to Elizabeth about it, told her about the money, said a great deal about the money.

'I'll be away for two months but we'll have money for the rest of the year. It will be an easy life for us, you can be here with James, take him to the church school. We've got some money left from the sale, so you can stay with the captain's wife. You'll be a lady of leisure.'

Two months became four, then six, as we scoured the bloody coast under the command of Captain Evans. The money was good for the rest of the year but Elizabeth was angry that I had left her alone for so long. The Government had given her a letter saying I had to take up the new thirty-acre grant or lose the land. The plot that they gave me was further back from the river, but had been underwater like mine. I took it all the same and with the first sealing money had a house built. Elizabeth and me, we stayed with Thompson until it was ready. I didn't work the ground, for I was frightened nothing would last if I did. I would walk my land, pull the ivy away from trees, watch the green and red parrots climb the sky to squabble in the branches. Some days I would hunt duck. We came to live on Thompson's charity for soon I had nothing to give him.

He had more voyages for me. Along the coast and across to Van Diemen's Land, longer and longer each time. Captain Evans hired McIntyre and he hired Williams as a favour to me, for John Williams had barely spoken a word since we dragged him out of the river. Years were measured by hunts not harvests. Thompson wasn't married, Elizabeth kept his house for him, and the conversation on my returns between them was too easy for me. I disliked too his growing friendship with my son.

The last time I was back, my house was good and ready, with two floors and a porch, but Elizabeth wasn't living there. She was still in Thompson's house, telling me she was too frightened to live alone. Doyle told me that by then the natives had all been rounded-up, put in chains, taken to some island to die. None were seen spear-fishing in their canoes, walking with their dogs. I took Elizabeth and James and all her things to my house, we were strangers there. I fixed-up the leaks, painted the front door, heated it. The bed was slept in for the first time.

'Are you going to farm now?'

'No,' I said, 'too late to sow.'

'You could make the ground ready.'

'I need to rest don't I? We need to live in this house. I've been living on a boat, on rocks and beaches. It's good to be home, and see James.'

We ate and slept together but did not embrace. James' was often the only voice in the house. I played with him but otherwise my days were idle again.

'What good is a farm if you don't grow anything?' she asked.

I put in some vegetables, but I couldn't muster the will for crops. Land had been unfaithful to me.

When spring came round again, Thompson came to me.

'I've bought my own boat, the *Speedwell*, she's called. And Evans has found a rich vein of seals, he's been given a map.'

'How long?' I asked.

'Short journey, I'd say, couple of months. But the take, the take is going to be better for everyone because I'm not paying to charter the vessel. Bigger cut for all see. Interested?'

'I have a farm again now.'

'You've no seeds in the ground and no crop to harvest. This'll see you through the year Ruse.'

I told Elizabeth it would be my last voyage, that when I returned we would have another child. She looked no happier, nor sadder, than when

I had left or returned before. I told her to live in our house from now on. I kissed her and I kissed my son goodbye.

CHAPTER 22

The Wrought Sea

We were hopeful at the beginning, Williams and me. The natives did not give chase for they wanted the sealskins more than they wanted us. The island disappeared from view and the smear of the mainland darkened. The open water did not make us fearful, the craft held off the spray and the sky was promising. McIntyre and Scottish Jack were not spoken of. I knew why John Williams had killed McIntyre and I do not condemn him for doing so.

We thought we might be at the mainland the following day, but then as darkness fell we seemed to cross a threshold to another sea. The water billowed all around, pulled at us from underneath; a west wind gripped the canopy we had made. When dawn came, the mainland had gone. I steadied the boat so that John could stand and he saw only the surging waves.

'North!' he cried.

We rowed, rowed … rowed, yet progressed as far eastwards as we did north.

Three nights have passed since Scottish Jack saved us but in my mind I see only the water barrel fall to the ground, not the man. I have drunk my own water, Williams would not drink his. He stopped rowing yesterday, lay down, and spoke his final words.

'I had the run of it in London, for a few years. Sneaks every day into houses, Clerkenwell, Smithfield, pockets in Cheapside, I could do a lot of tricks. But I was noticed, someone like me with a bob or two gets a name, gets a foot on the gallows. I was lucky they didn't scrag me as a boy, a couple of my chums were. I got too cocky, got nabbed one day fleecing a washing line. In Virginia men were as wicked with me as they wanted to be. When I came back, my brand gave me away. I hoped it would be better in New Holland. Safer for the likes of us. I was going to bring-up the boy so that he wouldn't know what it was to be whipped. Would have taught him so that he never gave anyone the cause. If new Holland is going to be the place James, then it is better off without McIntyre. Don't you think?'

I nodded, but he had closed his eyes. Some time after he gave up the ghost. He is at rest now. I have never seen his face as such. His life was like this voyage, at the mercy of nature and man's nature, for man is like the land and the sea, resenting the rule of others, and having to be tamed and tended to. Some I have known have done this well. They were fortunate that they fell amongst good men, and good soil. Some of us, we fell on stony ground, and have failed to thrive, and I being left now to the mercy of God and the sea.

The Man They Couldn't Hang

A Tale of Murder, Mystery and Celebrity
by Michael Crowley

W WATERSIDE PRESS

A play in two Acts with a captivating introduction by the author. The true story of John 'Babbacombe' Lee is one of the most bizarre in criminal history. Lee is the only person to have to have cheated the gallows after the trapdoor failed to open. This happened at Exeter Prison in 1885 when the notoriously inept public hangman James Berry gave up after three abortive attempts. Lee spent 22 years in prison before being released. On retirement, Berry, who carried out 134 executions, wrote *My Experiences As An Executioner*. His resulting celebrity led to him taking to the boards, spinning gruesome tales of his former trade and showing audiences his dark souvenirs. Michael Crowley's imaginative play is set in a down-at-heel northern music hall where the proprietor is bent on reviving the venue's glory days by persuading the now released John Lee to team up with Berry in a perilous double act.

'This work would undoubtedly provide a wealth of meaty material for any drama workshop worth its name, whether inside or outside of the prison wall. I hope to have the opportunity to see it performed some time, if only to have a good laugh at a good (or rather bad) hanging'
Prison Service Journal

Paperback | ISBN 978-1-904380-64-1 | 2010 | 140 pages

www.WatersidePress.co.uk

Behind the Lines

*Creative Writing with Offenders
and People at Risk*

by Michael Crowley

With a Foreword by Lord Ramsbotham

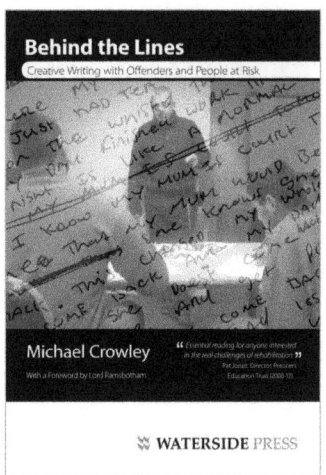

Behind The Lines is the product of some 15 years of working with offenders and people at risk in prison and in the community. It is based on the author's extensive experience of using creative writing to change and improve thinking and behaviour to prevent crime. It includes: Easy to read explanations of the method; Dozens of practical exercises and ideas for discussion; Advice about the different approaches; Samples of writing by offenders, inside and outside of prison; The author's views about what works to engage and encourage (often) wary participants. *Behind the Lines* represents a major contribution to rehabilitative work (it is the prison-writing equivalent of the highly successful Waterside Press publication, *The Geese Theatre Handbook*). A Key Resource for: Offending behaviour group workers; Youth workers; Youth offending teams; Community workers; Psychotherapists, therapists and counsellors; Special needs workers and teachers; Writers in residence; Anyone tackling literacy levels of risk groups… and people training or studying in these and related fields.

'Essential reading for anyone interested in the real challenges of rehabilitation'
Pat Jones, Director of the Prisoners Education Trust (2008-12)

'Shows how you can turn the lead of anger and despair in prisoners into the gold of insight and creativity'
Oliver James, author

Paperback | ISBN 978-1-904380-78-8 | 2012 | 256 pages